INDIAN MUMMY
MYSTERY

Some Other Books by Franklin Folsom

EXPLORATIONS OF AMERICA

THE FIRST BOOK OF INDIANS
        (*Pseudonym*, Benjamin Brewster)

THE FIRST BOOK OF ESKIMOS
        (*Pseudonym*, Benjamin Brewster)

THE REAL BOOK ABOUT INDIANS
        (*Pseudonym*, Michael Gorham)

THE REAL BOOK OF GREAT AMERICAN JOURNEYS
        (*Pseudonym*, Michael Gorham)

BEYOND THE FRONTIER (*Fiction*)

THE HIDDEN RUIN (*Fiction*)

SEARCH IN THE DESERT (*Fiction*)

SAND DUNE PONY MYSTERY (*Fiction*)

MYSTERY AT RUSTLERS' FORT (*Fiction*)

THE DIAMOND CAVE MYSTERY (*Fiction*)

THE STORY OF ARCHEOLOGY IN THE AMERICAS
        (*co-author* Mary Elting)

EXPLORING AMERICAN CAVES (*For adults*)

A WILDERNESS MYSTERY

INDIAN MUMMY

MYSTERY

by Franklín Folsom

with illustrations by

JOHN J. FLOHERTY, Jr.

HARVEY HOUSE, Inc., *Publishers*

Irvington-on-Hudson, N. Y.

© 1962 by Franklin Folsom
Illustrations © 1962 by Harvey House, Inc.

Library of Congress Catalog Card Number: 62-10796

This is the clothbound Library Edition of
the book which appeared in a popular
edition as INDIAN MUMMY MYSTERY
by Troy Nesbit.

MANUFACTURED IN THE UNITED STATES OF AMERICA

Contents

CHAPTER 1   Ghost Town

Joe Cutler and Denny Grogan lounged on the back porch of the Rocking O ranch house, which lay well back from Highway 160, in southwestern Colorado. From where the two boys sat they had a good view of a swinging footbridge across Blue Monday Creek. On the other side of the creek stood a cabin that the Cutlers rented to summer visitors. There in the middle of the bridge was a woman, holding onto the handrails for dear life.

"Harold!" she screeched. "Ha-a-rold! You've got to come and get me."

A boy who looked to be about fourteen dropped a bundle on the far side of the creek, gave a bored glance at the woman, then trotted down the swaying, bouncing bridge toward her. Every step he took joggled her a little. Obviously the new boy had not yet caught onto the trick of walking smoothly over the bridge. Once he lurched against the protective wire netting that hung between the handrails and the planks that made the footpath.

"Ha-a-rold!" the woman squealed again. "Be careful. You'll kill us both!"

Joe and Denny grinned at each other. The bridge was perfectly safe, but you had to know how to catch the rhythm of it with your steps if you wanted to get across without being thrown off balance. Joe and Denny always enjoyed watching the antics of tenderfeet on their first trips over Blue Monday Creek.

"Quit your yelling, Ma," the boy on the bridge said, as he glanced with embarrassment at the audience, Joe and Denny, in their box seats on the porch. Grabbing his mother's arm, he ushered her clumsily to safety. Then he escaped back across the bridge toward the old station wagon in which he and his mother and father had arrived from their home in Denver a little while before.

As if by common understanding, Joe and Denny slouched to their feet and walked through the kitchen and dining room to the front porch.

Joe was tall for his fifteen years—five feet eleven, and he was still growing. Already his big wrists stuck out of the sleeves of his sweater, which had on it the letter A he had won playing basketball at Alamosa high school. Denny was almost a foot shorter, two years younger, and on the chubby side. Neither of them said anything, but they were both sizing up the new boy to see if he would be of any use to them. They were apparently going to be stuck with him for the summer. His parents had rented the cabin right through from this last week in June until Labor Day.

On the front porch Joe and Denny joined Grandpa Cutler who was looking through a mail order catalogue The boys squatted down near him and began to take some trout flies from the hatbands of their Stetsons. They had gone fishing after an early breakfast and now had to put the flies away in boxes. Out of the corners of their eyes, they watched the new boy swing a knapsack from the tailgate of the station wagon onto his back. It was obviously heavy and he staggered a little as the weight fell across his shoulders.

Grandpa Cutler slammed the catalogue shut and walked noisily across the porch in his high-heeled cowboy boots. At the corner he called to the newcomer, "Hi, partner, had chuck yet?"

"What did you say?" the boy asked, looking up at the

old man in surprise.

"I said are you hungry?"

The boy's face broke into a grin. "I sure am."

"I just happened to notice that there's a cherry pie stand-ing out in the kitchen. Help yourself," the old man said.

The boy looked tempted but uncertain.

"Come on in," Joe mumbled and opened the screen door. He was glad that his mother had never been able to break Grandpa of the old ranch habit of offering food to strangers.

In the kitchen the three boys all helped themselves to generous slices of pie and ate it in silence. Then Denny's bright blue eyes shone mischievously out of his round face. Grinning, he pointed to a hand-lettered sign over the kitchen door that read:

If you can't wash dishes, don't eat.

Denny and Joe started breezily toward the swinging door while the new boy pondered a moment. They paused and looked back. The boy stared at the three dirty plates, shifted the knapsack he still had on, picked up only the plate he had used and gave it a quick dousing under the

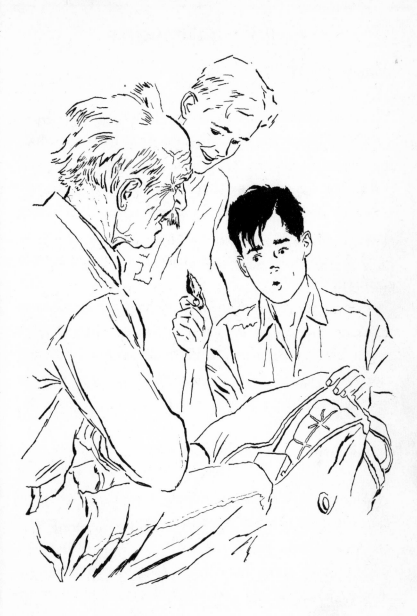

cold water faucet. Then he turned to the boys and said, "Good eating."

Joe and Denny grinned appreciatively and went back to wash their own dishes. They began to feel some hope that the kid would not be a dead loss around the place, although it looked as if he might need a little taking down.

"I'd better make you acquainted," Grandpa said to the new boy when Joe and Denny filed back silently to the front porch with him. "My monicker's Lyman Cutler, but I don't like being called Lie for short, so people generally call me Fibber. This long drink of water is my grandson Joe, and this barrel-shaped buckaroo is Denny Grogan."

"Harold is my name," the new boy said, "Harold Hansen, but people who want to get along with me generally call me Huff."

Joe and Denny grunted "Hi," and it looked as if the conversation had come to a dead stop.

Making a valiant effort to get some talk started, Huff asked, "Are there any minerals around here worth collecting?"

Joe and Denny looked at each other. It was clear that Huff *would* need some whittling down to size.

But Grandpa said, "There was a time when they took a whole lot of silver and gold out of these hills," and he jerked his thumb toward the jagged La Plata Mountains that shot up only a few miles away. "Time was when I used to do a little prospecting myself up Coyote Canyon there."

Huff was all ears. "Do you think I might find something if I went up that way?"

"Oh, sure," the old man said. "They say there's still as much silver in the Fourth of July mine as has ever been taken out. But I'd advise you to be careful. I got into an awful fix in that canyon once."

Joe and Denny knew exactly what was coming. They squatted down on the edge of the steps to enjoy the whole thing.

"I was up there alone," Grandpa continued, "when a band of Ute Indians happened along collecting souvenirs like you do. Only difference was they specialized in scalps, and mine was the only one handy. I had a fine curly head of hair at the time and I was mighty choice of it. So I decided to hike on about sixty miles an hour, keeping a wee mite ahead of the Utes. I was making out all right till I turned off and found I was in a box canyon."

"What's that?" Huff asked.

"That's the kind of canyon there is only one way into and no way out of, if there happen to be bloodthirsty Utes following you with their bows and arrows all ready," Grandpa answered. "In other words, it's a canyon with walls straight up and down on three sides. I kept on till I ran smack into the end of it. And there were the screaming, painted warriors right behind me."

Grandpa paused, took off his battered four-gallon hat, and reflectively ran his fingers through the gray tufts of hair that stuck out of his head like little rabbit tails.

"What happened then?" Huff asked, just the way he was supposed to.

"Why, they killed me," the old man answered mournfully.

For just one instant Huff hesitated. Then he swung the knapsack down from his back, opened the top, and burrowed deep down in it with one arm. In a moment he straightened up with something clutched in his hand. Opening his fist before the old man, he said, "I wonder, does this happen to be the arrow they did it with?" and he gave an elaborate wink at Joe and Denny.

Grandpa studied the arrowhead carefully. He turned it

over and ran a finger along the jagged edges. Then he announced with great dignity, "Yes, partner, I believe this is the very one."

Joe and Denny poked each other. Huff was doing all right.

"What else you got in that sack?" Denny asked.

"Well, I have a rock that can catch fish," said Huff.

"That's better than these two did this morning," Grandpa said, pulling his ragged mustache and pointing to Joe and Denny.

Huff burrowed into the knapsack again and brought out an odd-shaped piece of rock that was black and heavy-looking. He waved it over the fish hooks that Joe had left lying in his open tackle box on the porch rail. The hooks leaped up at once and stuck to the black rock.

"Neat!" Denny exclaimed. "What is it, anyway? How does it catch fish?"

"You just saw it catch fish hooks, and fish hooks catch fish, don't they?" Huff said, as if it was beneath his dignity to have to explain anything so obvious. Then he added, "It's stuff called magnetite. That's a kind of iron ore that's magnetic. I didn't find it though. There isn't supposed to be any of it around here. I had to buy it in a specimen store when we came through Durango."

"You got anything else?" Denny asked again.

Huff began pulling things out. First came a squirrel's tail and a comic book, then a cracked china cup, the top of which was partly covered. Grandpa gave a snort when he saw it.

"Where in tarnation did you get that mustache cup? I haven't seen one of those since I was knee-high to a prairie dog."

"I found it in an old shack yesterday way up the other side of the pass in a place called Pair-a-dice. That's a ghost town."

"We have a ghost town right here on our ranch," Joe said.

Huff looked up. He was cautious about rising to Joe's bait. "What kind of stuff can you find there?" he asked.

Suddenly, Joe was as much interested in the question as Huff. "Come to think of it, I don't know. This is only my second summer here, and somehow I never thought about looking for anything."

"What's the place called?" Huff asked.

"Canary City," said Denny. "That's because the prospectors around here used so many Rocky Mountain canaries to pack their stuff. That's what they called their burros," he explained. "Say, why don't we go over and have a look?"

"Nuts, you know I can't go now, Denny. I have to do up the cabins and fill the wood boxes before Mom gets back from town," Joe said. "Of course, if you guys want to help—"

Denny was usually very good at missing the point of a broad hint like that, but today he had a good reason to lend a hand. The trip to Canary City might be worth while.

So, while Denny found brooms for himself and Huff, Joe got fresh linen from a closet in the ranch house. It was his job every day to take care of the Cutlers' six tourist cabins. Ever since his father had died, more than two years ago, Joe and his mother had lived here with Grandpa on the Rocking O Ranch in the summertime, running a tourist camp. Grandpa was getting too old to run the place by himself. So, besides letting his daughter-in-law take in tourists, he leased his pasture land to Denny's father. Grandpa just took care of riding horses for tourists, milked a couple of cows, and, under protest, fed some chickens. Today, tourists had rented all the horses, so the boys would have to hike a mile and a half to Canary City. This was all right with Huff. He admitted he did not know one end of a horse from the other.

It was soon clear to Joe that Huff did not know any more about using a broom than he did about horses. So Joe put him to work splitting kindling wood. But that was no good either. Obviously Huff had never had an ax in his hand before. Then Joe told him to stuff the dirty sheets and pillowcases into the laundry bag. He could not go wrong on that. Much as Joe hated making beds, he had worked out a system of doing them well enough to pass his mother's inspection. He sped swiftly ahead with that job.

Just as they were nearly through the last cabin, the boys heard a shrill voice calling "Ha-a-rold!"

"Thar she blows," grumbled Huff with a shrug, but he went running.

Joe had visions of another long delay before they could get started on their expedition. But Huff was back in no time, saying, "Well, what's holding us up? She just wanted to know whether I'd fallen in the creek and got drowned, or something. She likes to worry. Anyway, my father said I could go with you to the ghost town."

On the way across the wide pasture that lay between the ranch house and Canary City, Denny warned that this first trip might not come to anything.

"It's only safe to go near Canary City when Old Tom isn't around," he said. "He just plain doesn't like visitors —sort of a hermit. He's the only one who lives there. People say he would just as soon fill your Levis with lead as not."

"Does he own the place?" Huff asked.

"No, Fibber does. But he lets the old boy live there," Denny answered.

And then he told Huff the rest of the story. Back in the late eighteen-eighties, when Canary City was a booming mining camp, Old Tom's father, whose name was Swink, started a general store there. One day the whole town burned down, and just about the same time the boom ended. So the place never got built up again. The miners lived in tents for a while, then everybody moved away but Tom. His father had died in the fire, and Tom had sort of turned hermit. Years later, Grandpa Cutler bought the whole place for taxes and turned it into pasture. But by that time Tom was a fixture. Grandpa felt sorry for him and let him stay in the shack he had knocked together out of old timber.

Old Tom shot an occasional mountain lion and did a little prospecting for silver in the mountains in summer. He believed in the old saying, "A good silver mine is above timberline, ten times out of nine." In the winters, he made a little cash for himself by doing something he learned from Mexican sheep herders. He braided horsehair into hatbands and McCartys.

"What's a McCarty?" Huff wanted to know.

"It's a lead rope tied to the bosal just in front of the hackamore knot," Joe answered.

"Is that anywhere near the carburetor?" Huff asked innocently.

Joe and Denny burst out laughing. "It's just a good strong rope that you tie to the halter when you want to lead a horse," Joe said. "Cowboys used to swear by horsehair ropes. They put them in a ring around their bedrolls at night because the horsehair was supposed to keep rattlesnakes away. The ones who didn't get bit by rattlers claim it was the McCartys that saved them."

A mile and a half of walking had brought the boys to a little rise from which they could look down at the ghost town. It did not amount to much. Just a few rows of rock foundations where buildings had once stood, Old Tom's weatherbeaten shack, and one particularly large heap of rubble at the foot of a stone wall, one story high. All of the buildings had once hugged the foot of a mountain that rose up steeply right here out of the flat pasture land.

There was no smoke coming from the hermit's cabin as they approached. That probably meant he was away. Still, the boys were cautious as they went past his place. They headed for the big pile of rubble by the high stone wall.

"My pop told me this is where Swink's store used to be," said Denny.

Joe had been feeling a little glum after his first look at the ghost town. You really could not call it a town of any kind. There was not a single building left except Old Tom's shack. Weeds and grass were growing everywhere. It did not look as though there were any interesting relics to be found. But when Denny mentioned "store," Joe had an idea.

"Do you suppose there's stuff still buried in there?" he said.

"No," said Denny. "If there was anything worth-while left, somebody would have got it long ago."

But Huff was not so sure. He had made a find in a ghost

town where hundreds of others had doubtless explored before him. He pointed to Old Tom's cabin and said, "Let's borrow that shovel over there and dig around a little."

"Sounds to me like that's borrowing trouble," Denny said.

"Come on, Denny," Joe said. "As long as we're here we might as well try."

Taking turns using the short-handled prospector's shovel, they soon had dug away the weeds and grass and a thin layer of dirt that covered part of the heap. Then they began to pull away stones that had once belonged to a wall. It looked as if one side wall of the store had collapsed during the fire. Under the stones, they found some pieces of charred wood, and bits of broken glass.

Denny was beginning to get bored when Huff let out a yell. "Boy, look at this." He held up a mud-caked, old-fashioned brass padlock. This gave Denny new hope and he helped dig farther.

Joe uncovered something that looked as if it had been part of a clay dish. He could just make out a sort of design on it, and he guessed it might have been part of an Indian pot. He was going to throw it aside, but instead he slipped

it into the hip pocket of his Levis.

Then Huff's eye caught something special. He picked it up and saw that it was a nest of amethyst crystals. He doused it under Old Tom's pump, scratched the dirt away with a small stick, then polished it on his baggy gray sweater. Now he could see the whole shape of the purplish-colored quartz crystals.

"Gee, this will be a good specimen for my collection," he said.

Just as Huff started to poke around some more, Denny gave a shout. "Yowee! Dough! Look at this." He held up something that was the size of a fifty-cent piece, although it was so black with tarnish that they could not make out anything on it.

Denny had started to rub the object clean in the grass when Huff happened to look up and saw a man with a burro coming their way across the pasture. "Who's that over there?" he asked quickly.

"Uh-oh!" Joe answered. "Old Tom. Seems to me I hear our mothers calling. Everybody says the old boy's crazier than seven hundred dollars. We'd better clear out."

Joe grabbed the shovel, ran to the shack and stood it in its place. Then the three of them lit out at a fast walk, making a wide swing through the pasture so as not to meet the hermit.

When he saw the boys near his shack, Old Tom gave an excited shout and began beating the burro, trying to make the beast hurry. As the boys looked back over their shoulders, they could see him throwing stones futilely in their direction, shaking his fist at them, and letting out his anger on the burro which just would not hurry.

The boys were glad enough when the rise in the meadow was between them and the angry hermit. Now, as they approached the cabins and ranch house, Denny had time to examine his coin again. It had been rubbed clean enough in his pocket so that he could see it was a fifty-cent piece. Right off, Denny could think of half a dozen ways to spend it, but Huff said:

"I wouldn't spend it right away if I were you. It might be worth a lot more than fifty cents, because it's so old. There are guys that collect coins and they're willing to pay plenty."

"Neat!" said Denny with enthusiasm. "How'll I find out?"

"I saw a bunch of old money in the window of the store in Durango where I got my magnetite specimen," Huff answered. "They'd probably know there if the coin was valuable."

One thing was sure, the boys all wanted to return to Canary City as soon as they could.

CHAPTER 2   The Stolen Mummy

When Joe and Denny reached the swinging bridge, they told Huff to come over to the ranch house after supper. Then they went in and found it was later than they had thought.

"You look like coal miners. Wash up, Joe," said Mrs. Cutler cheerfully as she backed through the swinging door to the dining room with a steaming dish in each large, strong hand. "You, too, Denny. Your mother phoned a little while ago and I told her that I'd feed you if you showed up."

"Howdy," the boys said to three tourists who were sitting at one table. They sat down with Grandpa at another. They knew from long experience that the old man held firmly to the cowboy belief that meals were for eating and not for talking. They would have to wait until after they had done the dishes before they could tell him about their

29

discoveries at Canary City.

Either by luck or by careful calculation, Huff arrived in the kitchen just as the last dried dish was being put away. He still had his knapsack on. Together the three boys made for the sitting room where Joe and Denny knew they would find Grandpa reading yesterday's *Denver Post*. Mrs. Cutler sat at an old-fashioned roll-top desk figuring up bills and writing checks.

"Hey, neat!" Huff exclaimed as he looked around the sitting room. Almost every inch of space on the walls and floor and the ceiling, too, was covered with hunting trophies, animal skins, Navaho rugs, and old-time photographs. An enormous stuffed and varnished trout sat on top of the roll-top desk.

Huff's interest and surprise reminded Joe how he had felt himself when he saw the room for the first time. It was fun to answer the questions he knew Huff was going to ask.

"This is the skin of a mountain lion Grandpa shot on our front porch one winter when the snow was four feet deep," he said. "That grizzly bear hide came from up Coyote Canyon. Grandpa caught that trout when he was about my age, in a lake near Creede. The biggest ones now aren't even half that size. That's a wolf skin. There used to be a lot of them around here, but now we only have coyotes."

"What's that?" Huff asked, pointing at a queer-looking wastebasket near the desk.

"It came from an armadillo," Joe answered. "Grandpa got it in Texas one time."

"Look, Fibber," Denny broke in, and he held out his fifty-cent piece. "I found it over where the old store used to be at Canary City."

Grandpa took the coin and examined the figure of Liberty stamped on it. "Four bits," he said. "Old, too. Eighteen-sixty-one." Then he turned it over and exclaimed, "Uh-oh! Sorry to disappoint you, Denny. This isn't worth any more than the silver that's in it—if there is silver. It's just plain Confederate money. Maybe you've heard the saying 'It's not worth a Confederate dollar.' And this is only half a dollar."

"Do you mean it's as bad as counterfeit money?" Denny sounded brokenhearted.

"I guess that's about it," Grandpa answered.

"Tough luck," Huff commented.

"Keep it for a lucky piece," Joe said comfortingly.

"We'll go back and look some more. Maybe somebody lost a real piece of money or something through a crack in the floor."

"I found an amethyst specimen that's a beaut," Huff broke in, pulling it out of his pocket and holding it up to the light.

"We dug around a little in the old store ruins," Joe explained to Grandpa.

"You might find more specimens there," Grandpa said. "I remember now that Swink used to keep his front window full of ore samples and Indian curios and that kind of stuff."

"That's probably how this happened to be there, then," Joe said. He reached in his pocket and took out a piece of the broken pottery that had a small fragment of a design on it.

"Say," Denny interrupted, "I bet there is a lot of money that got left when the store burned down. I'm going back as soon as Old Tom goes on a trip and dig it all up. Maybe we'd find enough to buy a jalopy, boy. Joe could drive it on the ranch roads, and pretty soon he'll be old enough to get a driver's license and then we can go on a camping trip. . . ."

"I don't like to spoil your trip, Denny," Grandpa said, "but I don't think there's money in the store. I'll tell you why. The fire that burned down Canary City started in Swink's place on a Monday morning. Swink was up at the bank depositing all the cash he'd got over the week end. He left some hombre to take care of the store while he was out. It might have been one of the no-goods who hung around there a lot, and he must have been drunk, because all of a sudden he started emptying his six-shooter. The way we figured it, one of the bullets must have hit the kerosene lamp Swink always kept burning at the back of the store where the light wasn't so good. At any rate, people began to yell fire pretty soon. When Swink saw where the fire was, he rushed into the store to try to save something. In a couple of minutes he was crawling back, half burned up, and he didn't live the day out. Tom, his son— that's Old Tom the hermit—saw his father die, and he never got over the shock of it. The Canary City volunteer fire department only had a hand pump, and for all the good it was, they might just as well have tried to put the fire out by spitting on it. The whole town was gone in no time."

"You mean every single house in the place burned up?"

Huff asked.

"Sure," said Grandpa. "There was a high wind and all the houses were built of wood, except the store, that is. It had two stone walls, and even one of them got pulled over when the second-story beams burned through. I can remember how the place used to look as plain as anything. It was built right into the hill, and the back part just had a dirt floor. That was the part where Swink sold meat. The front had a wooden floor."

Denny's mind was still on his disappointment about the fifty-cent piece. "Are you sure Swink went to the bank with all his money, Fibber?" he asked.

"Yep," Grandpa said. "Oh, maybe he kept a little in his till for making change. But I'll tell you what—there's something you might find, if by a miracle it wasn't busted in the fire. That would be an Indian pot of a certain kind. They were worth something in Swink's day and now they're worth a lot more. He always had one or two showing in his window or in a glass case inside. Let me see that thing you have there, Joe."

He took the fragment of pottery and looked at it for a moment.

"No, this isn't the really old stuff. The kind I'm talking

about was black and gray. It came from the cliff dwelling ruins in Mesa Verde. Cowboys used to rummage around those ruins, and if they found pots they sold them for whatever they could get. Nowadays museum fellows just water at the mouth whenever they run across one of the real old-time pots."

Joe knew about Mesa Verde, and he had been wanting to go there. It was only forty-five miles away, but somehow last summer they had always been too busy with the tourist cabins, and they could not get away. He had seen plenty of pictures of the mysterious towns that Indians had built long ago in caves, high up in cliffs. The government had made the place into a National Park, and tourists could go right into the ruins now and look at them.

"Speaking of that," Grandpa said, "I had some of those pots myself one time, and I might have sold them to Swink if I'd kept them long enough to do it. But I had a little accident."

Joe suspected a story was coming—one he had never heard before. "Yeah?" he said helpfully to lead Grandpa on.

"Another young fellow and I had to ride range in that

part of the country, looking for calves that hadn't been branded. I was just about your age, Joe, at the time. We worked up Soda Canyon on the south side of the mesas, dabbing the Rocking O brand on quite a few calves that had been born after regular branding time. If rustlers found unbranded calves, they just appropriated them, and we wanted to make sure that none of ours got taken that way.

"By late afternoon, we'd worked into a side canyon when we saw a little bunch of ruins in the cliffs that didn't look hard to get to. We'd heard all about the ruins around there from some cowpokes named Wetherill. They were three brothers who discovered the cliff dwellings in the first place, and they'd made quite a little thing of collecting curios that the Indians had gone off and left in their houses, nobody knows why.

"My partner and I figured we might as well look around for some stuff, too. Cowpunchers sometimes found beads or arrowheads or a queer kind of sandals in the houses, but mostly they went in for what they called pots. A pot was any kind of dish or jug that the Indians made out of clay.

"Well, we climbed up a place where there were regular

footholds dug in the cliff wall, and we got into the cave. There were a lot of little square rooms built out of stones around the back of the cave, and right in the middle of the cave floor there was a hole that led down to an underground room.

"We poked around in the rooms, and sure enough, we found pots. Some of them weren't even cracked or broken. We picked up four or five of the best ones in the lot, and then we noticed something that looked like a doorway at the back of one room. It had been filled up with stones. Just for the fun of it, we pulled the stones out, and we found that another room had been built behind the first one.

"It was too dark to see anything, so we lit a piece of juniper wood for a candle, and crawled through the little door. And then we saw the queerest thing. It was a bundle all wrapped up in a strange kind of blanket made of feathers. Inside the bundle was a real, honest-to-goodness mummy."

Grandpa paused and lit his pipe.

"And what did the mummy say to you?" Huff asked with a grin.

"Keep still," Joe said. He knew his grandfather well

enough to distinguish between a "windy" and a true story. "Why didn't you ever tell me this before?"

"I'm seventy-seven years old," Grandpa said mildly, "and you'll be pretty near that old before I've had time to tell you everything that's ever happened to me."

"Well, go on," Denny said impatiently. "What happened then?"

"So, there was Bellyache Bill—that's what we called the mummy right away, because he had his knees all drawn up to his chest and his arms folded, just as if he had a champeen bellyache. We handed him out of the room mighty carefully, so as not to bust him. Then we cooked ourselves some supper and left him to scare off the varmints while we took forty winks.

"Next morning we bundled him up nice and comfortable in one bedroll and tucked the pots away in the other. Then we went on about our business, which was mainly heading back home.

"I guess I should have mentioned that the horses we were riding were top cow ponies. Anywhere they went, they were likely to attract the attention of fanciers of horseflesh, and our pack animals weren't just half-broke mustangs fresh off the range, either. They were broke to the

saddle, too, so altogether we were as tidy a little outfit as you'd find.

"It appears we weren't the only ones that thought so. Just as we got out of the side canyon into Soda Canyon, an hombre on a chestnut mare appeared out of nowhere all of a sudden. We found ourselves looking into the barrel of his shiny new 'persuader.' My partner and I had rifles, but we didn't have time to reach for them before we found our hands hoisted pretty well above our heads and likely to stay there."

"You mean this guy was a robber and held you up?" Huff asked.

"Robber's not the word for it, son," said Grandpa. "He was a rustler and a horse thief. Without so much as a howdy-do, he set us afoot and shooed us on down the canyon toward the Mancos River. We were a good forty-five miles from home, with nothing but our cowboy boots to hike in and no food to eat. It took us two days and about a thousand blisters on each foot before we got back here to the kitchen."

"Didn't you ever get the horses back again?" Denny asked.

"What about the mummy Bellyache Bill?" Joe wanted

to know.

"We never saw the ponies again, nor Bellyache Bill nor the pots. We kept our eyes open, too."

"Did you ever find out who the robber was?" Huff asked.

"*Rustler,* I said. We never saw him again, that we knew of, but we couldn't be positive. He slid his bandanna up over his nose as if he didn't quite like our smell, and otherwise he looked pretty much like any other cowpoke. Still, I always figured he was part of the Stockton-Eskridge gang. Some of them were suspected of hanging around Canary City once in a while. At any rate, as I already mentioned, rough characters used to hang around Swink's store.

"The gang finally got pretty well shot up in a street fight in Durango. For all I know, the coyote that made off with our horses that day might have been hurt in that very fight."

Joe couldn't get the mummy out of his mind. "I should think it would have been easy enough to trace the mummy," he said.

"I thought so, too, at the time," Grandpa replied. "Traveling shows and museums bought up mummies whenever cowboys found them in the ruins. I asked the Wetherills if they ever had word of Bellyache Bill—they knew about all there was to know about everything that came from Mesa Verde. And they were pretty sure that Bellyache Bill had never gone into general circulation. It's one mystery story that never got solved, and it always made me kind of sorry."

Just then Mrs. Cutler rattled down the roll top of her desk, locked it decisively, and said, "That's all of Grandpa's stories for tonight, fellows. Joe, you better get the kitchen kindling for morning. I'll drive Denny home, it's so late. Here's a flashlight, Huff. You'll want it going across the bridge."

Mrs. Cutler was like that, managing things smoothly, and not acting the least big high and mighty. Briskly she shooed Denny out the door and into the pickup truck and headed off down the main road to the Grogan ranch house a mile away.

Denny was the youngest of seven children. There were so many big boys and girls at home that, if he did not get around to doing his chores, it did not make very much difference.

After Joe had brought the kindling into the kitchen, he

went upstairs to his room. Then he lay awake for a long time, wondering about that mummy. Could it be possible, after so many years, to solve the mystery of what had happened to it?

CHAPTER 3 A Real Find

Joe hustled through his chores the next morning. He had finished cleaning all but one cabin before Denny arrived. The tourists in that cabin were sleeping late, and Joe fumed about them to his mother as she worked in the kitchen. She had told him he could take the rest of the day off, as soon as his work was done. Now it looked as if those tourists might sleep till noon.

"I'll tell you what, Joe," his mother said at last. "I'll do that cabin if you'll save me time by counting out the laundry right now."

Ordinarily Joe was some place else when that boring job had to be done. But now he began with real enthusiasm to pull dirty sheets out of the big hampers in the closet under the stairs.

"Mom," he called after a while, "have you seen anything of that new kid this morning?"

Mrs. Cutler looked up for a moment from the pie crust she was rolling out on the table and glanced through the kitchen window toward the Hansens' cabin across the creek.

"He's around, all right. And if I'm any judge, he'll be here as soon as he can get away. Right now his father seems to think he should chop some wood for their cookstove. Oh-oh! There goes the edge on the ax I left in their cabin."

"Huff's not a bad kid for a city fellow, but he sure doesn't know one end of an ax from the other," Joe said. "I found that out when he tried to split some kindling for me. Say, what about the Hansens anyway? I just barely saw Mr. Hansen when they came yesterday."

"I gathered from Mrs. Hansen that her husband wasn't very well. He's a schoolteacher in Denver, and he's come up here to rest and do a lot of reading and writing that has to do with his teaching job. That's all I know, except they seem like nice, quiet people."

"Quiet!" Joe exclaimed. "Did you hear Mrs. Hansen when she was crossing the swinging bridge?"

"Come to think of it, I don't think she's been over here since they arrived," said Mrs. Cutler. "Was she scared?"

Joe began to chuckle. "I bet we don't see her till fall and the creek freezes over so she can walk across on the ice."

Mrs. Cutler joined Joe with a big comfortable laugh. "When I went over to see if they needed anything yesterday, she did seem a little nervous. Here comes the boy now."

Joe was nearly through counting the sheets.

"But don't hold your breath till he gets here," his mother went on. "He started on a dead run, but he's stopped in the middle of the bridge. Now he's trying to see how far he can make it swing back and forth and up and down all at once."

But soon Huff, and Denny with him, clomped along the back porch and into the kitchen, just as Joe finished with the laundry.

"Hey, Joe, are we going to ride the horses today?" Denny asked.

"You ought to know we're not," Joe answered. "Buck took a bunch of tenderfeet off on them again." Buck was one of Denny's older brothers.

"Shucks," said Denny.

"It's not far, and Huff here doesn't know how to ride

anyway," Joe said. "That reminds me, we better take something to eat. Okay with you, Mom?"

"Sure, if you fix what you want yourself," his mother replied.

Joe went to the pantry and got a fresh loaf of homemade bread, a huge wedge of orange-colored store cheese, and a pound of raisins he saw on the shelf.

"Turn around," he said to Huff. He opened Huff's knapsack and poked the food down into it, halfway wondering if Huff even took the knapsack off when he went to bed.

When the boys reached the rise near Canary City, they all lay down and crawled forward so they could see Old Tom's shack without being noticed themselves.

"His jackass is still there," Denny groaned when he caught sight of the burro. "That means the hermit is, too, probably."

In a minute they saw Old Tom come out of his door and catch the burro. Then he put a pack saddle on it and began to tie a load on.

"Hot ziggedy! It looks like the old buzzard's getting ready to do some prospecting," Denny said, almost too loud. Then he groaned again. "There goes our shovel."

"Why didn't you think to bring a shovel of our own?" Huff said crossly to Joe.

"Why didn't *you* think of it if you're so smart?" Denny came back.

"We'll find something to scratch with," Joe said calmly, then added, "Tom's slower than that donkey of his."

The minute Tom disappeared up Coyote Canyon, the boys scurried across the pasture to the ruins of the old store. A board had been stuck into the hole which they had made the day before, and on it was nailed a brown paper bag with a penciled warning: KEEP OFF.

"Nice of him to leave us the board," Huff said. "We can probably use it for digging." He took off his knapsack and all three of them went to work pulling stones away and kicking around in the rubble to loosen the earth with their feet.

Denny's ambition to find enough money to buy a jalopy was still strong, in spite of what Grandpa had said. He sifted dirt through his fingers to make sure he would not miss anything as small as a half dollar. For a long time all he found were several rock specimens which he handed over to Huff. The specimens took Huff out of operation while he washed each one thoroughly under the hermit's pump and polished it.

"I know this is mica," he said holding up a piece of rock. "Look how you can pick off layers of it with your fingernail."

Denny straightened up to take a look. Then he saw the second specimen that Huff had washed. It had small chunks in it that shone with a yellow gleam. "Hey, fellows!" said Denny. "Gold!"

"A truckload of that stuff wouldn't buy a hot dog," said Huff. "It's fool's gold. I know because I've already got some in my collection. Anyway this is a good specimen and I'm going to keep it."

Huff wrapped the two stones in the paper bag that Old Tom had left and put them in his knapsack with as much care as if they had been fragile bird eggs. Then he went back to digging.

Joe had been pulling aside rocks and heaving handfuls of dirt away, but his mind was only half on the digging. He wished he had lived when there were real discoveries to make—like the ones the Wetherill brothers had made at Mesa Verde, and like his grandfather had made when he found the mummy. Besides, the other boys had had all the luck so far.

After they had lunched on their bread, cheese, and raisins, Joe's hand probed into a hollow place under a couple of stones that were braced together. In there he felt something round and smooth, like a small bowl. Working very carefully, he lifted the stones away. It could be just an old sugar bowl or an ordinary piece of Indian pottery. But it might also just happen to be one of those precious Mesa Verde pots.

At last he had made an opening large enough so he could lift the object out into the sunlight. It was an Indian bowl, all right, and it was black and gray, but he could not be sure whether it was the valuable kind or just an imitation.

"Look what I found over here," he called, full of sudden excitement. "Maybe it's one of those Mesa Verde things."

"I bet it is," Denny shouted. "I bet it's worth two hundred dollars at least. We can sell it to a museum and get a jalopy."

Joe had to laugh. "You and your jalopy." At the same time he shared Denny's passion for an old car. He knew just how he could soup it up if they could get one of their own.

Huff said nothing and turned quickly back to the place where he had been wrestling with a big chunk of something. He kept so silently busy there for a few minutes that Denny came over to see what was going on.

"Hey!" Denny called to Joe who was sitting and admiring his pot. "Come! Huff's got something too big to move here."

Joe saw that what they were trying to move was a large, deeply charred block of wood which was wedged among some stones.

"This must have been Swink's butcher block," he said as he lifted more of the stones away. "The stones and mortar falling on it must have kept it from burning all up in the fire."

Joe and Denny gave a backward heave on it, almost losing their balance as the block gave way and rolled toward them.

In a flash, Huff was bending over the hole it exposed. "Wow! Lookit!" he said. And when Joe and Denny saw his startled expression they didn't need a second invitation.

For a moment all three stared, and no one spoke. Then Denny reached down and pulled out a skull, a human skull.

"Let's see that," Joe said. He examined it gingerly. The back part of the skull was broken and pieces were missing. "You know what—I bet this is the skull of Bellyache Bill, or at least some Indian mummy. The back of the head is bashed in. Maybe he got tomahawked."

"Let's go home quick and give it to Grandpa to put in the sitting room," said Denny.

"Hey, it's mine," Huff said.

"I picked it up from the hole first, didn't I?" Denny came back at him.

"I saw it first, and that's where I was digging. You just reached in and grabbed it out from under my nose." Huff was not quite sure of his rights, though. The other boys would probably stick together. He looked questioningly at Joe.

Joe was not paying much attention to the squabble. This had to be the skull of Bellyache Bill, and the sixty-year-old mystery would be solved. At first it did not occur to him to wonder why the mummy would be under the butcher's block, but he did have a pretty good idea why the skull had not been burned to powder in the fire. It had been protected by the butcher's block and by the earth floor under it. Falling stone and mortar had obviously kept the block as well as the skull from being burned to ashes. Joe came out of his daydream as Huff said,

"Joe, it *is* mine, isn't it?"

"You two quit arguing," Joe said. "Let's see if we can find the rest of the mummy."

Suddenly Huff and Denny felt a little squeamish. But they did help Joe who began systematically taking away more of the rubble. Next to the place where the skull had been was the jawbone. Then Joe picked out other bones and parts of bones.

After another minute or two, Denny said impatiently, "Let's go home now. I want to show the skull to Fibber right away."

Joe was anxious to go, too. He had found the Indian pot and now they had the skull. The whole thing seemed to add up. The rustlers must have brought Swink the things they stole from Grandpa.

"All right," he said. "Huff, take your stones out of the paper bag, and we'll put the skull in. You can carry it in your knapsack."

Huff did as Joe told him. "I can keep it, can't I, Joe?" he said.

Before Denny could explode, Joe answered, "If it's the

mummy, it belongs to Grandpa. If it isn't, I guess you should have it. It was your idea to dig here, and you really did see it first."

Suddenly a gleam came into Denny's eye. "Okay, you can have it till we get home," he said to Huff. "But I know one thing. Your mother will never let you keep it. And then you gotta give it to me."

There was a haunted look on Huff's face. He was sure Denny had something there. Still, he had found ways of getting around his mother before, and maybe he could do it again.

Joe knew Denny pretty well, and he was certain that a firm warning was indicated. "Denny, you have to promise something," he said. "You can't say even a word about this skull in front of Mrs. Hansen. If you do any dirty tricks so she finds out about it, we won't let you ever dig over here again."

"Okay, okay," Denny said. "There's probably lots of skulls buried here anyway." In a flash he was off on this big new idea.

As fast as they could, they started for home. Huff shouldered the knapsack containing the skull wrapped in the paper-bag KEEP OFF sign the hermit had left. Denny and

Joe, with his Indian pot in one hand, walked on either side of Huff, almost as if they were bodyguards.

When they reached the cabin on the way to the swinging bridge, Mrs. Hansen was hanging out clothes she had washed. She looked at Huff as if he had caught a bad case of leprosy.

"Harold Hansen! You go right out behind the house and take those filthy clothes off. You've ruined everything you're wearing. What in the world have you boys been doing?"

Joe looked at the others and then at his own blackened hands and clothes. He had to admit that Mrs. Hansen did have a point.

"We'll be washing up, too, Huff," Joe said. "When you finish, come on over to the house."

"No, Harold," Mrs. Hansen said. "As soon as you have made yourself decent, you and your father and I are going to Mancos to do our shopping. We'll have dinner there, so you have to stay clean. And tonight you're going to bed, young man. You stayed up till all hours last night."

"But what about the—" Denny started to blurt out about the skull, but he caught himself and finished lamely "—the—story Fibber was going to tell us?"

Huff heaved a sigh and shifted his knapsack a little self-consciously.

Joe could not see any way to relieve Huff of the knapsack. All he could do was hope for the best. Maybe Huff would leave it on the cabin porch, so that Joe and Denny could get the skull to show to Grandpa after the Hansens left for Mancos.

But forty-five minutes later, as they sat expectantly on the back steps of the ranch house where they could view operations around the cabin, the worst happened. Mr. Hansen came out and helped his wife across the bridge, holding her arm the whole way. Then Huff walked out of the cabin, swinging the knapsack onto his back, and strode across the bridge. He passed the boys with a big grin on his face that advertised his satisfaction. Denny could not "borrow" the skull during his absence.

"Harold," his mother said, "what in the world are you bringing that knapsack for?"

"It's the handiest way to carry the groceries," Huff answered, beaming.

"Not a bad idea," Mr. Hansen said. "Put it in the back." He opened the tailgate of the station wagon. "Now climb in and let's get going."

"That does it," Denny remarked.

"It sure does," said Joe. "It does it up double. I just hope Mrs. Hansen discovers her groceries have been cuddling up against a nice dirty old skull."

CHAPTER 4   Difficulties

Joe was on pins and needles. Last night he had shown
Grandpa the Indian pot, and Grandpa said he was sure it
was one of the genuine, old-time Mesa Verde pots. However, he couldn't be sure after sixty years that it was one
of those he had picked up along with Bellyache Bill. He
didn't seem to remember that any he had found were quite
that small.

Grandpa was just as eager as Joe was to see the skull.
He said there might just be a chance it had belonged to
the mummy—or *a* mummy at least. He could probably tell
by looking at the teeth. Grandpa had learned from the
Wetherills one interesting fact about the Mesa Verde Indian people. A grownup's teeth were always badly worn
down. That was because so much sand got mixed with
their corn meal. They made the meal by grinding corn
between two pieces of sandstone. Every time they chewed

a piece of their cornbread, sharp grains of sand filed away at their teeth.

Joe admitted he had not noticed whether the skull even had teeth in it. He and the other boys had handled it rather gingerly.

Huff was apparently having trouble this morning getting his mother's permission to come over from the cabin. Joe had finished his chores, and now he was at the barn where Grandpa was putting a new cinch on a saddle. The horses were all in the corral, and the three boys could ride over to the old store as soon as Denny and Huff showed up. Huff's father had asked Grandpa to let Huff learn to ride.

Joe was restless waiting for the others, and he was still annoyed at Huff for carrying off the skull last night. Now he itched for something to do. Half absent-mindedly, he began cleaning the spark plugs on the pickup truck. He always liked to tinker with the engine when he got a chance.

Finally, Denny shuffled listlessly into the barn and leaned against the big barrel that held oats for the riding horses.

"What's eating on you?" Joe asked.

"Plenty," said Denny. "My pa says I can't go over to Canary City any more."

"Why not?"

"Well, Pa met the hermit up the canyon yesterday. Old Tom was raving mad about us digging over there. Pa says he's afraid the old boy might be nutty enough to shoot us the way he says he will if he catches us digging around there again."

Joe himself had no desire to be shot at. "What do you think, Grandpa?" he asked.

"Old Tom's bark is a lot bigger than his bite," Grandpa said. "I wouldn't have let you go there in the first place if I thought he'd do any harm. In fact, I wouldn't let him live there at all if I thought he would hurt anybody. He likes to throw stones at people, but he always makes sure he's at least a quarter of a mile away when he does it. He's the one who's scared."

"So it's all right to go back over there?" Denny said cheerfully.

"You do what your dad says," Grandpa replied. "I'll tell him my ideas about Old Tom when I see him, but I don't teach kids to disobey their parents."

"But the hermit's gone off on a prospecting trip," Denny

protested. "I'll bet that he's away off up in the hills by this time."

"You can't be sure. He might have changed his mind and come back already. You fellows just use the horses today while you have a chance. Take Huff and show him how to ride, but stay away from Old Tom's side of the pasture."

"I wish Huff would show up. You still haven't had a chance to look at that skull," Joe said. Restlessly he picked up the big tin can that Grandpa used for dishing out oats to the horses. He slapped it back and forth in his hands as if it were a basketball. "Go see if you can't get him out of his mother's clutches, Denny."

Glad for something to do, Denny disappeared at once. In a little while he was back with Huff and the inevitable knapsack.

"Have you still got it?" Joe asked. He had been half certain that Mrs. Hansen would find the skull and make Huff get rid of it.

"Sure thing," Huff answered.

Joe dived into the knapsack without waiting for Huff to take it off his back. Then he pulled the skull out of its brown bag and handed it to Grandpa.

Grandpa turned it every which way and said nothing for a while. In the meantime Joe had taken the jawbone out and looked at it eagerly. The teeth did not look worn away, but he was not willing to give up all his hopes so easily.

Finally Grandpa broke the silence. "This is sure one interesting skull. It's not Bellyache Bill's, but there might be a connection at that. First of all, this hombre never chewed any sand with his cornbread, and sometime or other he had enough money to get this." He pointed to a back tooth that was capped with gold. "I never heard they had dentists in the cliff dwellings."

Both Denny and Huff wanted to know what teeth had to do with it. Joe explained.

"Now what do you make of this?" Grandpa pointed at a small round hole in the forehead.

Joe realized he had not noticed this either. Maybe it had been covered with dirt when they found the skull the day before.

Now he began to see what it was that Grandpa was getting at.

"Is it a bullet hole?" he asked.

"It isn't anything else but," Grandpa replied. "Look at

the way the bullet tore up the back of his head coming out."

"I thought that was where he got smashed with a tomahawk," Denny said.

"No," Grandpa said. "I never saw it before, but I always heard that bullets go into a head clean and come out messy. This sure proves it. And it proves something else. There was more going on in Swink's store the day of the fire than anybody ever guessed. Looks to me now like that fire was no accident. Whoever plugged this hombre must have wanted to give people something to take their minds off him while he made a getaway."

"What do you mean?" Joe asked.

"I told you people heard shooting in the store, and then the fire started. Well, there was shooting all right. This is how I figure it. There must have been two of those no-goods in the store that day. The fellow who pulled the trigger saw that he'd be in trouble as soon as Swink came back and noticed a corpse behind the meat-chopping block. So the gunman just grabbed the kerosene lantern, bashed it where the fire would spread fast, waited as long as he could to be sure it was burning good, and then ran out yelling 'fire.' Of course, we know the fire spread, and everybody was in too much trouble to worry about a tough character or two who didn't show up again."

Grandpa paused, thinking.

"Go on," Joe said.

"Nobody who lived in town was missing after the fire," Grandpa said. "So it never occurred to anyone that there'd been a murder. Swink died that same day, so if he knew anything he couldn't tell. It's ten to one that both this fellow—" he held up the skull "—and the coyote who shot him were part of the rustler gang that were supposed to hang out around Swink's store."

"Wow!" Denny stared wide-eyed at the skull in Grandpa's hand.

"Then this fellow could have been the very one that set you afoot in Soda Canyon," Joe said. "The one who stole your mummy and pots."

"Could have been. They were mighty grabby, those rustlers, what they did sometimes wasn't the least bit pretty—like what happened to whoever owned this skull. But you know, when you come right down to it, the rustlers were only a little bit grabbier than all the rest of us were.

"We just swiped the land from the Ute Indians in the

beginning. Then we dug for gold and silver under the ground and grazed stock on the grass above it. When fellows came along later and tried to grab our cattle or horses or our mining claims, we didn't like it. We called them rustlers and horse thieves and claim jumpers. Off and on, people got pretty rough. The rules about how to grab politely hadn't caught up with us. Sometimes things like this happened." Grandpa pointed to the bullet hole. "I didn't like it then, and I don't like it now. But I will say that if there was just half as much shooting and killing in the old days as you'd think from watching television shows there wouldn't be anybody left alive around here to tell stories.

"This fellow is actually the first one I ever saw who got plugged, although the Stockton-Eskridge gang didn't exactly run a Sunday school."

"Well, if rustlers hung out at Swink's store," Denny impatiently interrupted the old man's reflections, "then maybe they hid loot right there in the store. No telling what we might find there. Come on, Fibber, let's go have a look. You said yourself it's safe enough."

"Now you're the grabby one," Grandpa said grinning, "but I'll tell you what I'll do. I'll talk to your father and if he agrees, I'll go over with you. Anything you get there isn't going to hurt anybody."

"But he left this morning," Denny said with a note of desperation in his voice. "He's gone to look over the cattle up on the range. He won't be back for maybe a week or more."

"Swink's store isn't going to walk off in the next week. It'll be there when your dad comes back," said Grandpa.

"But we want to get over there and look for stuff," Denny insisted.

"You've got all summer to poke around there. You fellows give Huff a riding lesson now and worry about the store later on."

Joe felt as disappointed as Denny and Huff looked. Somehow his grandfather's sensible decision had taken all the excitement out of the idea of digging in the old store. When you had found the skull of a murdered rustler, you did not just teach a city kid to ride for a week and think that is all there was to life.

After a restless and dismal silence, something began to work in Grandpa's head.

"All this business is kind of giving me an idea," he said at last. "I've got a hankering to go back and take another look at Mesa Verde. How would you kids like to come along? I might even be able to show you the place where I found Bellyache Bill—that is, if those government dudes who run the place will let me."

None of the boys jumped at the idea. A trip was all right, but they had their hearts set on going back to Canary City. Huff was the first to show some interest, then a look of worry and uncertainty crossed his face.

"I bet my mother won't let me go," he said. "I'm pretty sure she won't."

"Don't worry about your mother. I'll talk to her," Grandpa answered.

"Well, all right," Denny said. "We can go over there and back by suppertime if we start now. We might as well get going."

"Hold your horses, Denny," said Grandpa. "The way I figure, we'll stay two or three days and make a real camping trip of it."

"I've never been camping," Huff said with a little more enthusiasm.

Grandpa was warming up to the scheme. "As I remember, there's a mummy in the museum that looks a little like Bellyache Bill, and some pots, too. But I don't know if they'd let you look at the best cliff dwelling, Denny. There's one tunnel you have to crawl through that's awful narrow."

"Quit kidding," Huff said.

"No, I mean it," Grandpa said seriously. "The guide actually measures broad people like Denny to see if they're likely to get stuck. I guess he'll make it, though. The regular tours are for dudes, but I think I can persuade the guides to let us go off by ourselves and do some real exploring. Every once in a while somebody makes some new discovery over there."

Joe began to see possibilities. He had wanted to go to Mesa Verde last summer, but there had not been time. The trouble was, he did not see how he could get off now. He had to help his mother every day taking care of the cabins. Grandpa guessed what was on his mind.

"We'll get that redheaded sister of Denny's to come over and help your ma," he said. "Let's plan to go Monday as soon as the week-end rush is over."

Joe gave a slap to the oats can that he still held in his hands. Then with a one-arm sweep over his head, he tossed it at the oats barrel, as if he were taking a shot in basketball. Now things did not look half bad.

"Even if Huff can't go, you'll take us, won't you, Fibber?" Denny asked.

"I have a hunch it will work out so we can all go," the old man answered.

CHAPTER 5   "Tell the Superintendent"

"That's the park entrance ahead," Grandpa said. "We have to stop and pay the man to get in." He leaned a little forward in the front seat of the station wagon, talking across Huff at Mrs. Hansen who was driving.

Joe was still a little surprised at the way arrangements had worked out. Mrs. Hansen had agreed to let Huff come on the expedition, but she had insisted on driving them all. She had pointed out that Mrs. Cutler might need the pickup truck. Mr. Hansen wanted to stay at the ranch and work, and there was no reason why she should not see Mesa Verde with Grandpa and the boys. Camping out was decidedly not in her line, but there were tourist cabins in the park where she could stay, while the others slept in bedrolls in the campground.

At the gate, the uniformed park official collected the entrance fee and carefully counted the number of occupants of the station wagon.

"Know why they count us?" Grandpa chuckled. "They keep careful track of how many people go into the park and put down the figures in one column. They count you again as you go out, and put those figures in another column. At the end of the summer they add up each column. If the sum totals are different, they know that somebody got lost during the summer. Maybe fallen off a cliff or something. It's a very accurate system. No guesswork about it."

Mrs. Hansen let out a little gasp.

Grandpa turned to the gateman who had been listening. "Isn't that so?"

The gateman nodded soberly.

"How many were missing last year?" Huff asked.

"Five and a half," the man answered.

"What do you mean 'a half'?" Denny said.

"Three full-grown tourists and five young ones," the man said.

Mrs. Hansen saw she was being kidded, but her smile was not very enthusiastic. She was edgy about driving in the mountains anyway, and from here on the road grew less and less like the streets of Denver to which she was accustomed. The old station wagon began to labor as it climbed the road that wound up a very steep mountainside. Soon they came to a place where the road cut across the face of a cliff. Grandpa saw that Mrs. Hansen was getting more and more nervous. When they came to a turnout with a spectacular view, he suggested that they stop and look at the scenery a minute.

"Wouldn't you like a rest?" he asked considerately. "I'll be glad to drive."

"Oh, would you?" Mrs. Hansen was obviously very much relieved.

Huff was delighted. With his mother in the middle of the seat, he could be next to the window and could look down over the edge of the road as they drove along.

In another half-hour they were well out on the top of the great plateau called Mesa Verde. It was actually a high table of land that ended abruptly in steep slopes or cliffs and was almost surrounded by low flat country. On the south, a series of deep narrow canyons ran far back into the great mesa, and here it seemed as if long high fingers of land stuck out into the desert. Cliffs dropped away steeply on three sides of these fingers.

A road sign pointed to the public campground, and in

a little while Grandpa stopped at a vacant parking spot near a stone fireplace. A table and benches stood close by, shaded from the brilliant sunlight by juniper and piñon trees. Dozens of other camp sites with fireplaces and tables were laid out in the area, although each one seemed isolated from the others among the trees.

"We'll stake out a claim for ourselves here," Grandpa said. "We'll leave our bedrolls by the table, and then take Mrs. Hansen down the road a little way to the tourist cabins."

"But is it safe?" Mrs. Hansen asked. "Won't somebody steal the things?"

"It's funny," Grandpa explained, "but people seem to lose a lot of their grabby ideas when they come in here. Anything that you leave on your own camp site is perfectly safe."

The boys unloaded the bedrolls that held clean clothes and everything else they needed for the trip.

Mrs. Hansen opened the small portable icebox that was kept in the back of the station wagon and got out some lunch and lemonade. As they ate at the picnic table, she kept looking at the red, hard-baked soil. "Why, it will be like sleeping on bricks, Harold," she said. "I think you'd

better come to the tourist cabin with me."

Huff gave a desperate look at the old man and the other two boys. Grandpa came to his rescue.

"I'll show Huff how to make a comfortable bed," he said. "If he hollows out a place for his hips, he won't notice that the ground is hard. He'll sleep all right. I'll see that he makes his hip-hole, don't you worry."

"That's so, Mrs. Hansen," Joe said. "The hip-hole is the secret of sleeping on the ground."

"I suppose you know best," Mrs. Hansen said doubtfully. "You're sure there aren't any snakes?"

"Aw, come on, Mom," Huff said. "Let's get going."

After Mrs. Hansen had rented a tourist cabin and left her things in it, they drove to the park headquarters building. Grandpa told them that was where all the guided tours started, and the museum was there, too.

"Hop out, boys," Grandpa said as he stopped in front of the low, sprawling building. "You can see a mummy in there and a lot of other stuff, too."

Joe and Denny dashed on ahead, and when Huff caught up with them, they saw he had put on his inevitable knapsack. Grandpa and Mrs. Hansen stopped at the information desk to ask when the next tour started, and the boys scurried into the museum, looking for the case that held the mummy. In a minute they found it—a huddled-up figure, leathery and shriveled. They stared through the glass case in silence, studying it. Here was somebody who had actually lived on the mesa more than seven hundred years ago. The mummy gave them a queer feeling that was half excitement and half awe.

Suddenly Denny said, "How do you get to be a mummy anyhow?"

"I think they sort of pickled them in something," Joe answered.

"No, I don't think so," Huff said. "My father told me it's the climate here that does it. The air is so dry it just naturally makes mummies."

"I sure wish we could find Bellyache Bill," Joe said. "I can just imagine how Grandpa felt when he discovered him."

"Say, speaking of that, what did you do with our skull?" Denny said to Huff.

"I've got it right here—what do you suppose?" Huff answered, indicating the knapsack.

"You're crazy," Joe said. "Grandpa said we'd be climbing up and down places in the ruins all the time. You might bang it into something and bust it all to pieces."

"It'll be all right," Huff said. "I had to bring it with me. I couldn't think of any place to leave it where it would be safe."

"Why in the world did you do that? Now you have to find some place to cache it. Go on back to the station wagon and leave the knapsack there."

Grudgingly Huff agreed and went out of the building to the car. He had scarcely left when Grandpa came up and said:

"The trip to Balcony House is about to start. Where's Huff? You have to drive a little way to get there. Huff's mother will take you. I'm going to stay here and talk to a fellow I know. I'll see you when you come back. I don't mind saying I'm not as spry as I used to be. I have to save up my strength for tomorrow so I can show you where I found Bellyache Bill. The ranger will tell you about the ruins anyway."

Mrs. Hansen bustled up to them. "Where is Harold?" she demanded.

"He's already gone over to the station wagon," Joe said.

But in a moment Huff ran panting to join them with the knapsack still on his back. He saw Joe's questioning look and said, "Don't worry. Just take it easy."

"What did you say, Harold?" his mother asked.

"Nothing important," Huff said with a grin. "Where's everybody going?"

Joe slyly felt the knapsack. There was nothing in it. Joe began to worry. He hoped that Huff had not left the skull where Mrs. Hansen would be sure to see it. But when he looked in the station wagon there was not a sign of the paper bag.

Huff knew perfectly well what was going on in Joe's mind, and Denny's, too. He grinned with malicious satisfaction. But he was not going to spoil his fun by telling.

A whole cavalcade of tourist cars started out, led by the ranger guides. After driving a couple of miles, they stopped. There, close to the road, a great canyon yawned. It dropped straight away from the flat-topped mesa, and the bottom of the canyon lay five hundred feet below. All around, up to the edge of the cliff, gnarled juniper and piñon pines seemed to be growing out of the very rock of the mesa. Here and there a tough, scraggly rabbit bush clung to a little patch of soil, and spiky yucca plants stuck their sword-like leaves up fiercely.

Across the gaping canyon a broad bare band of yellow

rock showed under the fringe of dull green at the top. The surface of the mesa seemed to jut out over the perpendicular cliff walls.

Joe and Huff, and even talkative Denny, fell silent at the tremendous view. Joe and Denny had climbed mountains and had the bursting feeling of triumph at being in high places. But here was something different. Here every growing thing seemed to boast in its own twisted, thorny, defiant way that it had the strength to live in a place where living was one long thirst. The very roots here had to battle against solid rock.

Yet in this desert-like spot, hundreds and thousands of Indians had once made their homes. By looking carefully across the canyon, the boys could see the dark squares that were doors in stone houses the Indians had built in caves in the sheer face of the cliff. Joe wondered how in the world they had ever managed to carry stones and pile them up skillfully in such a difficult place.

Down at the drab-colored bottom of the canyon, Joe saw a wavy line that looked like a footpath and a tiny figure walking on it. "Is that where we go?" he asked one of the rangers.

"No, we don't go down nearly that far," the ranger explained. "Balcony House is right here below us. What you see at the bottom is a Ute Indian trail. That's a Ute walking on it now. He's probably looking for a strayed horse. The reservation is just over there," he said pointing. Then he added, "The Utes never go near the cliff dwellings, by the way. They think it's bad luck to go where people have died."

Now the two rangers began to herd everybody along a well-constructed trail down a steep slope until they were about a hundred feet below the rim of the mesa. Then the trail narrowed and went along the face of the cliff. Soon the boys found themselves on level ground under a great overhanging rock.

"Yipe! Look at that!" Huff pointed to a ladder ahead. It was almost as tall as a three-story house.

The ranger stopped the party and gave a little speech. The Indians built their houses in the cliffs for safety, he said. Ladders were often the only way in to the dwellings. In case of attack, they could be pulled up. Sometimes the Indians used foot and handholds dug in the rock, too. Sometimes they must have got into the caves by using nothing but a rope. Then the ranger added:

"This ladder here is safe and new. But it's thirty feet

high. If anybody thinks he's likely to get dizzy on it, now is the time to go back the way we came. The rest of us will meet you on top. We won't be coming back this way. We'll use another exit at the other end of the cave."

Mrs. Hansen gave a horrified look at the ladder. So did an elderly couple. The three of them decided to go back up the trail.

Then the ranger said, half-joking, "I have to look the rest of you over and make sure none of you are too fat. There's a narrow tunnel we have to crawl through." He held his hands out, pretending to measure Denny. "We'll send this fellow through last. Then if he gets stuck in the tunnel, he won't keep all of the rest of us from getting home."

Denny laughed along with everybody else. He was used to being kidded about his shape. The three boys were first in line to follow the ranger up the broad ladder. Huff and Denny climbed side by side.

"Don't look down while you're climbing," the ranger called. "Keep your eyes on the wall straight in front of you. Then you won't get dizzy."

Nimble though the boys were, they found the climb was not easy, but it was exciting. Behind them lay an almost

sheer drop of hundreds of feet. A great mass of rock bulged out above them.

At the top of the ladder they stopped in sharp amazement. There stood the ruins of a whole little town. The buildings lined the back of the cave. Along the edge of the cliff a low wall had been built. And between the wall and the houses was a courtyard.

The boys could have spent the rest of the day there, poking into the tiny rooms where Indian families had slept and stored their food, examining the round underground chambers, called kivas, where religious ceremonies had been held. Best of all was the tunnel which had been the ancient entrance to the cliff dwelling. It was fixed in such a way that one single person could defend it from a whole raiding party. The ranger was right about it, too. The cliff dwellers must not have been very large people, because Denny had an uncomfortable feeling of tightness when he crawled through on his hands and knees.

Exciting though the place was to them, the boys felt disappointment about one thing. All the rooms were absolutely bare. There was nothing new for them to find here.

"Are there any cliff dwellings that haven't been explored?" Joe asked the ranger.

"Lots of them," he answered. "Of course, we've been into all the main ones, but we aren't even sure how many hundreds of little ones there are in this area. Every once in a while somebody spots a new one high in the cliffs that we hadn't noticed before."

Reluctantly the boys left when the time was up. As they reached the top of the mesa they realized they were very thirsty.

"I can see what Huff meant when he said the climate here made mummies," Joe said. "I'm all dried out already. I wonder if there's any lemonade still left in your mother's icebox."

Huff gave him a queer look that made Joe suspect he had made off with the last of it. They sauntered on under the blazing sun toward the station wagon. When they got close they saw a large group of people had crowded around it.

Then somebody called out, "Hey, one of you boys go and get a ranger."

"What's the matter?" Denny asked.

"A woman here has fainted."

Just at that moment, one of the rangers came up, and

the three boys followed as the crowd opened to let him through.

"Oh, Mom!" Huff cried out in a sudden panic. His mother was lying stretched out unconscious on the ground by the roadside.

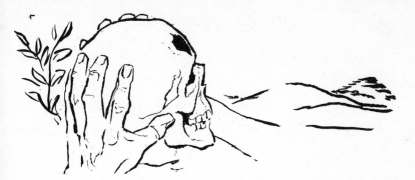

CHAPTER 6   **"It Won't Bite"**

"Don't worry, kid," the ranger said reassuringly to Huff. "The altitude was probably too much for her. "I've got an ammonia capsule that will bring her around in a minute. Stand back, everybody."

"Do you have a canteen in your car, sonny?" asked a bystander.

"There's ice in the icebox," Joe said quickly.

"Wrap up a piece in a handkerchief and give it to the ranger," the bystander directed.

Joe turned to the rear of the station wagon, where the tailgate was already let down. The lid to the ice compartment was open, and beside it lay a paper bag with KEEP OFF lettered on it!

"Thunder!" Joe gasped out—louder than he meant to. He hesitated.

"Hurry up, kid," somebody urged him as he stood motionless in front of the icebox.

With a shrug of resignation, Joe reached in, lifted something out, and placed it on the tailgate. It was their precious skull, which he had to move in order to get at the ice underneath.

The whole picture of what had happened flashed through his mind in an instant. Huff had chosen the ice compartment as the most likely place to hide the skull temporarily. Mrs. Hansen, seeing that their tour was finished, had started to get lemonade ready for them. (Huff, of course, had not counted on his mother's getting back to the car first.) To make the lemonade good and cold for them, she had probably decided to take out a chunk of ice. When she opened the ice compartment she saw the strange paper bag, opened it, let the skull fall back onto the ice and—*pffft!*

Now someone else saw the skull. Joe had been so flustered he had not thought to conceal it again in its paper bag.

A murmur went through the crowd, and their attention shifted to the strange phenomenon of a skull that had come out of an icebox. As they muttered in astonishment at this new development, sniffs of the ammonia began to revive Mrs. Hansen. She opened her eyes slowly and looked around in bewilderment. Then she raised herself up on one elbow, shaking her head a little as if trying to straighten out her thoughts.

Just then a big man, bustling with importance, snatched up the skull and elbowed his way toward the ranger.

"Something's going on here, Mr. Price," he boomed at the ranger. "Look what was hidden in that car."

Mrs. Hansen gave a helpless little scream and covered her face with her hands.

Denny, who always blurted out the first thing that came into his head, said, "Be careful of that thing, mister. It's ours."

The thoroughly surprised and confused ranger named Price stared at the skull and at Denny. Then he looked around for Huff who seemed to belong to the woman who was so upset. Huff had quietly edged his way through the people toward Joe.

Now Mr. Price jumped to his feet and took charge of things briskly. "I want those boys and anybody else who belongs in this car to stay right here," he said. "It's a serious offense to steal anything out of the ruins. Please, everybody else get in your cars and leave. The lady is all right." Taking the skull from the big man's hands, the ranger shooed people on their way.

After helping Mrs. Hansen into the station wagon, he glared at the boys with real anger. "I don't know how you kids were able to steal this skull, but you've got yourselves into a pack of trouble. You're on government property, and everything found here belongs to all the people in the United States—not just to you. Now you're going to the park superintendent. He'll see that you get what's coming to you. On the way we'll take this lady to the first aid station. Now hop in the back seat."

"We can explain everything," Joe tried to say.

But Mr. Price cut him off. "You'll have plenty of time to explain later."

The ranger got in beside Mrs. Hansen to drive the car. He set the skull in his lap for safekeeping, and zoomed off down the road.

Mrs. Hansen huddled in the corner of the seat, weak and bewildered, moaning, "Oh, dear me. Oh, dear me."

Their next stop was the first aid station, where the nurse told Mrs. Hansen she would be all right if she rested a while. Then the ranger shepherded them toward the headquarters building.

"Hey, Fibber! Grandpa!" Denny and Joe called out to-

gether with relief as they caught sight of the old man sitting on a shaded bench.

The grim young ranger started a little at the sound of their voices.

"That's my granddad," Joe told him. "He knows about the skull."

The ranger did not answer Joe, but he said to Grandpa as they came up, "Are you connected with these boys?"

"That depends," Grandpa answered, trying to size the situation up. "If they've been rustling cattle, I never saw 'em before."

"This is nothing to joke about," the ranger said. "If you know these boys, please come along with me. I'm taking them in right now to see the superintendent. They are charged with stealing government property."

"Please do come along, Mr. Cutler," Mrs. Hansen said, and it was the first connected sentence that she had uttered.

Grandpa had begun to get a serious look on his face, but Joe pointed at the skull the ranger was carrying like a football in the crook of one arm, and he winked at the old man.

"Oh!" Grandpa said. "I'll gladly come along. If these rapscallions have been up to any of their thieving tricks,

I'll help get up a party to run them out of town."

Looking harassed, the ranger ushered his captured criminals and witnesses into the office of the park superintendent. There, in a room lined with scholarly books, sat a man in a green park uniform. Pushing back from his desk, he looked up pleasantly and said,

"What can I do for you, Mr. Price?"

The ranger laid the skull on the superintendent's desk, triumphantly, as if he were making a touchdown. Then he explained the facts as he saw them. While the ranger talked, the superintendent was turning the skull over in his hands and examining it.

Now Mrs. Hansen seemed to pull herself together and broke into the story suddenly. "I found that thing in the icebox in my car. I was so frightened that I fainted dead away. I can't imagine how it got there, and I'm sure these boys don't know either."

"But the fat boy said distinctly it belonged to him," Mr. Price said in a firm, accusing voice.

"It doesn't either," Huff protested. "It belongs to me. If you'll just *let* me, I'll tell you all about it."

The superintendent looked up and caught Grandpa's eye. There was the faintest hint of a smile on the face of each of them.

"Remarkable, remarkable," the superintendent said drily. "A cliff dweller's skull with a gold tooth and a bullet hole in the forehead."

"Sir?" the ranger murmured. He leaned over and with a look of utter confusion and embarrassment inspected the gold tooth.

"Now which one of you young men wants to come clean?" the superintendent asked.

"*I* picked it up first—" Denny began, but Huff interrupted.

"Let me tell it straight," he said. Then he gave the whole story from beginning to end. "I knew the skull would bother my mother," he finished, "so I tried to keep it where she wouldn't see it."

As Huff talked, Mrs. Hansen stared wide-eyed at the skull. Then, surprising both boys and herself, she gave a nervous little giggle and said, "I suppose it really won't bite."

All except Mr. Price let go their suppressed laughter, and even he relaxed enough to say, "I guess the joke's on me, too. Sorry I stirred up such a fuss."

"It's a good thing to take your job seriously," said the

superintendent, getting up from his desk to show them they could go. "I hope you're feeling all right now, madam," he added to Mrs. Hansen. "And I hope you won't discourage your son from digging. That's how we archaeologists have found out a great many important things." Then he turned to the boys with a twinkle in his eye. "But if you find anything here in the park, I guess you know by now not to put it in cold storage. It belongs to Uncle Sam."

"That wasn't true when I came here in the nineties," Grandpa said. "A lot of us young cowpokes made off with considerable loot."

The superintendent gave him an interested look.

"Not that I kept any of what I found," Grandpa went on. "A rustler took it all off me in Soda Canyon. There was a mummy in the lot, and these boys have come over to find it again."

"What's this?" the superintendent said. "Tell me about it."

Grandpa related the story as the superintendent walked down the long hallway with them to the main entrance. Huff was the last one out of the room. He was putting the skull back into his knapsack.

The superintendent shook hands all round and said to the boys, "Let me know when you find that mummy. I've just told Mr. Cutler that you have my permission to look around."

CHAPTER 7

The Hidden Cave

Grandpa was no fool. He dug his hip-hole and laid out his bedroll that night at one side of the camp site. Then he told the three boys to get themselves settled as far away from him as possible. He did not want to be kept awake by the talk he knew would go on.

"I don't care if you fellows gabble all night," he said. "But you have to do it quietly. And no high jinks. There are folks camped all around us, and they got rights."

Following Grandpa's instructions, Huff used a stick and his heel to scratch a trough in the hard earth at just the place where his hip bone would come when he lay down in his blankets. Then he opened up his bedroll and stretched it out flat on the ground.

"What you got those things for?" Denny said, pointing to the pajamas Huff's mother had put in. "Don't you know that you're supposed to sleep in your clothes when you're camping out?"

Huff looked a little doubtful at first, but he followed the example of the others, thoroughly enjoying himself. He took off his shoes, put them under his head for a pillow, loosened his belt and settled down. With a delighted sense of discovery he found that he was quite comfortable on the hard ground. The hip-hole did the trick.

"I'd like to get a job here, digging in these ruins," Joe said. "It would sure beat sweeping out tourist cabins."

The other boys agreed. They had heard one of the rangers give a talk at the campfire program after dinner. He said that expert diggers worked just the way detectives do, finding out all about the people who lived here a thousand years ago. In addition to the houses in the caves, which were easily seen, there were hundreds of others buried under the earth. The experts even went through the Indians' ancient garbage piles, sifting the dirt through sieves. Joe could just imagine the fun of discovering beautiful turquoise jewelry, or weapons that had been used in battle five hundred years before Columbus. He was fascinated by the way one could tell the exact year a cliff dwelling had been built, just by studying a cross section of a wooden beam in a house.

Experts even learned from the beams the reason why the Indians had moved out of the cliff dwellings. They had compared the rings in the wood of the beams with other tree rings in the Southwest and found that a twenty-four year drought began in the year 1276. The dry mesa country grew even drier, and at last the Indians had to leave.

"We better take a sieve with us when we go back to Canary City," Denny said. "I bet I could find some real money that way."

"The thing that gets me," Joe said, "is how they put all this stuff together. They take a lot of little things and make a whole story out of it."

"Yeah," Huff said. "I never would have believed that those old Indians raised dogs for their hair the way people raise sheep. Did you hear the fellow say they made belts and ropes out of women's hair, too?"

"It sure is lucky the climate is so dry around here," Joe said. "But still I can hardly believe that a dog-hair belt or a turkey-feather blanket would last five hundred years."

"Well, they can have their turkey-feather blankets," Denny said. "I don't want them tickling my nose."

"And the way they figured out what happened to the people who used to live here!" Huff said. "It's just like a mystery story with clues and all. X marks the spot where the body lies."

After the other two had quieted down, Joe still kept thinking of the wonder of this detective work. If experts could piece together the story of an ancient vanished people, maybe it was not foolish of him to hope he could find clues that would lead him to Grandpa's vanished mummy. At any rate, they were going tomorrow to the place where Grandpa had found Bellyache Bill. The superintendent had given them permission to visit the cave, which was not one of the regular sightseeing places. With the cool fresh air of the night gently moving the piñon pine branches over him, Joe finally dropped asleep.

The next morning Mrs. Hansen gave them a map of Mesa Verde that she had bought. Then she put together a picnic lunch, complete with paper napkins, for Grandpa and the three boys. She planned to spend the day going on easy sightseeing trips where there were no ladders. "Don't worry about me," she said. "I've met a nice woman from Kansas, and when we get tired walking around, she and I are going to watch the Navahos who weave rugs and make silver jewelry up at the Lodge."

Joe went to the wash house at the campground and

filled four canteens with water from the tap. Grandpa put a package of raisins and four half-pound bars of hard, bittersweet chocolate into Huff's knapsack. (Denny had rolled the skull up in his bedroll for safekeeping.)

"I suppose those pink-tea sandwiches are all right," Grandpa said privately to Joe, "but this is the stuff that will get you there and back."

Then Mrs. Hansen drove them in the station wagon to the place where their hike was to start. The boys were surprised when Grandpa told her to stop very close to the spot where their Balcony House trip had begun yesterday.

At the rim of the canyon, Grandpa pointed across toward the opposite wall. "See that little black hole right next to a triangular slab of rock?" he said. "Well, that's where we're going."

"We saw that yesterday!" Joe exclaimed. "Why didn't you tell us we could see Bellyache Bill's house from here?"

"I thought you'd enjoy Balcony House more if you weren't always looking out across Soda Canyon," Grandpa answered. "Besides, I wanted to surprise you."

Soon they were scrambling down a steep gully at a place where there was a gap in the solid cliff wall. The gully took them to the bottom of the canyon. Grandpa's thin old legs had a hard time of it. Often the boys had to wait for him, but he scornfully refused offers to rest and take a breather.

All the way down, the brilliant early morning sun beat upon them. They took their jackets off and tied them around their waists. But at the bottom of the canyon they stepped into sudden shadow. It was cool here where the high cliff walls shaded them, and they were glad, because now they had to begin a scramble up a slope that was just as steep as the one they had come down. They were still in shadow when they reached a point directly below the cliff dwelling they were headed for.

Now it was time for a good long rest. Grandpa was very tired. Denny hinted that the boys might just as well go on ahead, but Joe rather sternly said, "No, we're all sticking together."

As they sat there, Grandpa pointed out to them a little side canyon where he and his partner long ago had hobbled their horses and left them to graze on a patch of grass that grew around a tiny trickle of spring water.

"We saw a spring right in Balcony House," Huff said. "Is there one in your cave?"

"No, there wasn't a sign of one when I was there,"

Grandpa answered. "The people must have brought their water up to the cave in pots."

"And right about there," the old man went on after a pause, "the rustler held us up."

"He must have been coming down the canyon," Joe said.

"That's right," Grandpa answered. "Let's go."

He led them toward a crevice that slanted upward in the direction of the cave. There the boys saw clear but shallow footholds and handholds that the Indians had pounded out of the rock with stone hammers. Full of anticipation they crept forward, keeping their full weight against the sloping rock as much as they could. The climb was fairly easy, and in a short while they hopped up onto the ledge that was the floor of the cave.

Suddenly, as they looked at the few small dwellings, they all felt a certain disappointment. Somehow they had expected this to be a very special place because Grandpa had found it. But there was nothing unusual here. In a few minutes they could see that the official explorers had not left so much as a broken piece of pottery.

"Where's Bellyache Bill's room?" Joe asked.

"Ought to be right through here," Grandpa answered.

"Give me the flashlight." Joe took it from Huff's knap-sack, and Grandpa flashed the beam into a bare little chamber at the back of the cave.

"X marks the spot," Huff said.

"Oh, shut up," Joe said. He stared around the empty cave, trying hard to think of something here that might be a clue. Try as he would, he felt farther from finding the lost mummy than ever, although he had expected that somehow he would be miraculously hot on its trail once he got here.

The letdown grew worse and worse, and all of them hated to show Grandpa their disappointment. They were glad when he said at last, "Okay, let's eat."

Although it was noontime, sunlight had not yet reached into the cave. They sat comfortably in the shade and gob-bled their dainty sandwiches and sucked the juice of the oranges Mrs. Hansen had packed in Huff's knapsack.

"Nice appetizer," Huff said. He broke a chunk off the big chocolate bar Grandpa had put in. But it was more bitter than the sweet milk chocolate he was used to, so he did not eat very much of it.

As they lolled around after lunch, Grandpa told them more about the days when he used to ride range in the canyon bottoms. He said cowboys hunting for pots used to make their camps in the underground kivas. The kivas had once all had roofs flush with the cave floor, but most of the roofs had caved in, leaving large round holes. The cowboys stretched tarpaulins across to keep in warmth and slept down in the kivas.

"I bet it was exciting in those days," Denny said.

"There was nobody around to make excitement," Grandpa answered, "except that one time when I got held up. Mostly it was just hard riding from dawn to dark."

"What are we going to do now?" Huff asked in a rather dismal voice.

"Grandpa," Joe broke in, "can't we hike on up the canyon a ways before we go back?"

"You young fellows can if you want to," Grandpa answered. "I'll leave you at the bottom of the canyon, and I'm sure I can hitch a ride back to camp."

"Let's go," Denny suggested. Action was what he wanted.

At the bottom of the canyon, Grandpa left them, saying, "If you don't take too long a hike, you can get a ride home with the last party that visits Balcony House. Otherwise, you hike along the road, and I'll come to meet you in the station wagon at just about suppertime."

The boys walked on to where the canyon divided. There they decided to take the right-hand fork. All the way, they were following the Ute Indian trail the ranger had pointed out to them yesterday. After about an hour, they flopped down on a little hummock to rest. There were no trees to shade them, and resting was almost as hot as walking. They had not seen any cliff dwellings they could possibly get to, and they had just made up their minds to start back when they heard a curious whining sound.

"Hey, there's a puppy some place," Huff said. "How in the world did he get here?"

"Pipe down," Denny whispered. "Wait a minute and we may see something. I bet it's a road runner."

Lying flat on their bellies on the hummock, the boys looked in the direction of the sound. Suddenly they saw a flash of gray among the clumps of low brush. Then it stopped, and they made out a queer, long-legged bird, with a tail that was as long as its body. The only thing that distinguished it from the dull surroundings was a fleck of red feathers near the eyes.

"Did you see that fellow run, Joe!" Denny exclaimed in a whisper. "I've been in the car when one of them tore along beside the road, just as if it were running us a race."

The streak of gray flashed ahead again, and then there was an explosion of activity in a patch of withered grass.

The animal's short wings beat violently, its tail wagged back and forth in the air, and a little cloud of dust appeared.

"I bet he's after a snake," Denny whispered. "Yeah! Look!"

They saw the tail of the snake lashing around.

"I hear that road runners don't eat snakes much," Denny said. "They just sort of kill them for exercise. Let's go look."

The boys moved up quietly, but the alert bird saw them and dashed away, leaving a small rattlesnake twitching on the ground. Joe picked up a rock and smashed the snake in the head. Meantime Huff and Denny were off after the road runner. The faster they went, the faster the bird traveled. It never took to the air, but ran with its small wings extended and used its long tail as a rudder. Joe joined in the chase, and they all ran until they were completely out of breath.

"Somebody ought to think of something useful to do with all that speed," Huff said from where he lay flat on

his back resting.

"Like what?" Denny asked.

"Like canning it and selling it for a million dollars to track teams."

"I'm starved," Denny said. *"And* thirsty."

All of them were. The bittersweet chocolate did not taste as bad now as it had when they first tried it. As they were washing it down with swigs from their canteens, Denny chirped, "Look, we've got company."

A young fellow, who seemed about Joe's age, dressed in Levis, work shirt, and cowboy hat, came down the trail. He was an Indian—a Ute, they guessed.

When he came close to them on the trail, the boys stood up and Joe said, "Hi." He wondered a little what response he would receive.

"Hi," the Indian boy said. "Are you on a hike?"

"Yeah, we got permission at the park headquarters," Joe answered. "We thought maybe we'd see some ruins up here that other tourists don't get to. We have to go back now. Do you mind if we walk along with you?"

"No, come ahead."

Huff and Denny were surprised that the Indian seemed so much like themselves. On the way down the canyon they found that he went to school in the winter as they did. Then Joe told him about their trip to the cliff dwelling where Grandpa had found the mummy.

"I've never been in the caves myself," the Indian boy said. "But I know where there's one that I am sure the rangers have never seen."

"Where's that?" Joe asked with interest.

"Less than half a mile from here. It's hidden by a big piece of the cliff that must have cracked loose so that it fell down right in front of the cave. I wouldn't have found it myself if I hadn't been looking for a short cut up to the top of the mesa once."

"Is it easy to get to?" Joe asked.

"I didn't try to go in," the Indian boy said. "But there must be a way."

"Will you show us where it is?" Joe asked.

"Sure," the Indian answered. And a little while later he pointed to a spot about halfway between the bottom of the canyon and the mesa top. All they could see from where they stood was a blank wall of rock. Below it, the ground sloped away sharply.

"If you go around to the left, you'll see a place where the big rock doesn't cover the cave all up. Maybe you can get in there," the Indian boy said.

After telling him good-by, the boys turned up the steep side of the canyon. Each of them was thinking that here was something really exciting. An unexplored cliff dwelling lay ahead.

CHAPTER 8   Work for a Human Fly

Joe's long legs took him uphill ahead of the other boys. He stopped at the foot of an almost perpendicular cliff. Directly in front of him was a great slab of rock that had obviously fallen in front of the cave. It was just as if a curtain had been pulled down, sealing the place off. Only at the far left side was there an opening that indicated a cave. And in the opening Joe could just make out some tumbled masonry of a cliff dwelling.

Whatever route the old inhabitants had used for getting into the cave had been hidden or destroyed when the huge rock fell down in front of it. There were no signs of footholds leading to the corner of the cave that was exposed. And the wall there seemed to be almost straight up and down.

Joe stared at the mere forty feet of rock that stood between him and the cave above. Here was his first big chance to do some real exploring, and he was stopped, absolutely.

"It looks like only a human fly could get into that place," Huff said as he came panting up to stand beside Joe.

Joe nodded, but he was determined to find some way into the cave. For twenty-five or thirty feet up, there were slight irregularities in the cliff face, and the edge of the great slab of rock was rough. Maybe, Joe said to himself, he could climb that far. He moved to one side for a better view of the last stretch below the cave floor. There was a ledge that ran across the cliff face, where one layer of rock seemed to join another. Above it, a depression in the cliff face ran up to the cave. This, together with the edge of the fallen slab, made a kind of chimney. Just possibly, Joe thought, he could inch his way up the chimney. At least he was determined to try.

"Here goes nothing," he said to the others suddenly. Stretching out his long body against the cliff wall, he felt around for handholds. There to the right on the slab was a good one. Now his left foot found a slight resting place. He heaved up and felt the rock all over with his left hand. Slowly he crept up, sometimes making only a few inches headway with each shift of his feet and hands. Sweating and quivering, he reached the ledge and relaxed.

"Here I come, Joe," Huff called.

"No, you don't. Not till I'm clear up," Joe replied. "I've got to see if it's safe first. Besides, if I kicked down any gravel or dirt in your face, it'd be good-by for you."

"Hurry up then!" Denny called back impatiently.

Carefully turning on the ledge, so that his back was pressed against the edge of the fallen slab, Joe lifted his right leg and found a place against which he could push the sole of his shoe. Tentatively he tried his whole weight on it, with only his foot and the friction of his back holding him. Then he found a spot for his left foot. He gave a little heave upward. Now he was wedged in the chimney, and moving only two or three inches at a time he began to work upward. Once when he paused a second to rest his aching muscles, he looked out over the deep canyon below him. A sudden hollow feeling struck his stomach and he got panicky. Quickly he turned his eyes back to the hard reality of the rock in front of him, and his confidence returned. Then, with every straining muscle taut, he made the last few heaves. His right arm swung over onto the floor of the cave, his right leg came up, and he rolled over to safety.

For a while he lay there panting. Then he sat up and looked around the place that he had struggled so hard to reach. At first his eyes, accustomed to the bright sunlight outside, could scarcely see a thing. But in a few moments he could pick out the dim outlines of the masonry walls of cliff dwellings.

"Joe!" Denny called. "What'd you find?"

Joe jumped to his feet and looked cautiously over the edge. Denny stood where he had left him, but Huff was already scrambling up onto the ledge, knapsack and all.

"Hey, you idiot, you can't get up here with that knapsack," Joe said in alarm. "You oughtn't to come at all."

"If you can do it, I can do it," Huff said between hard breaths.

"Doggone it, you can't!"

"Well, I'm going to."

"Don't be a pig, Joe," Denny yelled. "You got to let us come up."

"Hold on, then. Wait on that ledge and let me think," Joe answered.

In a moment, Huff looked up the chimney and saw Joe's Levis coming down toward him, but Joe was not in them. Then Joe's face appeared.

"Now listen, Huff," he said. "You take your knapsack off and be careful about it so you don't lose your balance. Tie it to my pants leg and I'll pull it up."

Huff did as he was told.

After Joe had pulled the knapsack up, he slid the Levis down the face of the rock once more. Lying flat on his stomach, with his arms hanging over the edge, and holding the top of the Levis, he was able to get the bottom of the pants legs down far enough for Huff to grasp them firmly.

Grabbing onto the Levis gave Huff the extra help and sense of security he needed while he heaved himself up the chimney. At the top Joe helped him roll over onto the floor of the cave.

Denny, in his usual impetuous way, had not waited for Huff to complete the climb. He had already started his scramble up to the ledge. He was waiting there when Huff's feet disappeared from sight at the top of the chimney.

Joe looked down and saw Denny's round, sweaty, beaming face below. "You haven't got the sense they promised a brass monkey wrench," he called irritably. "It's a wonder Huff didn't kick loose a heavy chunk of rock and bean you with it."

"Hurry up, Joe," said Denny cheerfully. "Send your pants down."

But the Levis were not quite long enough to reach him, for he was a little shorter than Huff. Joe had to knot the legs of Huff's pants to his own before Denny could get a good hold.

"Huff, you sit on my legs, so Denny won't jerk me off," Joe said. Then with an explosion of energy in his compact, round body, Denny began to surge up the chimney. Just as his hands were nearly over the edge so that Joe could catch hold of his wrists, a foot slipped and all his weight dropped onto the hanging Levis. The pull dragged Joe forward. Sudden fright filled him, and his fingers closed like vises on the blue denim he held.

There was no smile on Denny's face now, as his legs flailed around, feeling for some projection. His right foot caught onto a knob of rock and he gave a mighty heave. In a moment he had thrown the top of his body over the ledge.

"Okay, Huff, get off my legs and grab him!" Joe panted. With a final tug, Denny slid onto the flat, dusty cave floor.

All three boys were wringing wet from the exertion and

strain. Even Huff, who had not done much, was breathing heavily.

"My breath is coming in short pants," he said, chuckling and looking down at his bare legs, which were muddy from dust and sweat. "Give me my Levis, Joe."

"What's the use?" Joe answered. "We'll just have to take them off again when we get out of here in a little while. Come on, let's see what we can find."

He reached into the knapsack and brought out the flashlight.

As the boys turned their eyes from the brilliant sunshine that lit up only the small corner of the cave where they stood, they could see almost nothing in the deep, dim shadow behind the curtain of rock. The narrow beam of the flashlight picked out masonry walls at the back of the cave and shapeless heaps of rubble where walls had tumbled down.

"Look out!" Joe shouted suddenly as Denny started to walk toward the walls. He pointed the flashlight in front of Denny's feet. A great round hole gaped in the floor of the cave. In just two more steps Denny would have tumbled down about ten feet into the bottom of the ruined kiva. The roof of the kiva, which was also the floor of this part of the cave, had collapsed.

"Follow me around the back side," Joe said. "It looks safe enough here. But don't grab onto any of the walls. It looks like some of them might fall over if you just sneezed at them."

Beyond the kiva Joe flashed the light through one T-shaped door after another and saw nothing but rubble where the second stories of the houses had collapsed and fallen down inside. Then, as he looked in the door of one building which seemed solid, he whistled and turned around to the others who were right on his heels.

"Look at the pots! Here, Denny, you hold the light. I'll get them out."

Doubling up his long frame, he squeezed through the three-foot-high entrance to the room. There, close to the door, stood a large, wide-mouthed jug with another, shaped like a platter, sitting on top of it. Joe picked the platter up carefully and handed it out to Huff. "Now don't put it down some place and step on it," he directed as Denny turned the flashlight on the dish. "Hey, look. It's gray with the black markings on it that the old pots here are supposed to have. We sure got something."

Placing his hands around the base of the jug, he lifted

it with great care. "Say, this one's got something in it," he called out of the darkness. "Feels like it's full of junk."

As Joe passed the second vessel out, Denny flashed the light over it and started to grab at what was inside.

"Take it easy," Huff warned crossly. He had been impressed by the lecture the ranger had given the night before about the care scientists used when they excavated ruins. Handling the ancient pot as if it were an eggshell, he put it down and waited for Joe to come out.

"I just wanted a look," Denny said.

"All right, look, but keep your hands in your pockets," Huff said.

Denny turned the flashlight down into the wide mouth of the jar, as Joe bent over to look into it. There, staring him in the face, was a package of cigarette tobacco. Close beside it lay a packet of old-fashioned matches.

"Say, that's cowboy stuff," Joe said. "Let's see what else there is." He fished in and pulled out a pair of socks. Next came a shirt that looked as if it had been worn, and at the bottom of the jar there were two small bags of coffee and sugar.

"Some cowpoke must have left this cache here, maybe when he was out riding range the way Grandpa used to,"

Joe said. "Whoever it was must have intended to come back. The pots were worth something even in the old days."

"Let's take this stuff to the other end of the cave where it's lighter so we can see it better," Huff suggested.

Joe dropped the shirt and other things back into the jar. Then, with Denny holding the flashlight, and Joe and Huff carrying the two pots, they picked their way carefully through the debris toward the opening of the cave. When they got there, Joe looked out across the deep canyon and saw that the sun had gone down. Not only that, it must be a lot later than they had realized. They had been too excited even to notice that they were hungry.

"Listen, you guys," he said. "We're going to catch the dickens. It's probably after suppertime by now. We got to light out of here. We'll leave this stuff and come back tomorrow for it."

Joe knew that unless they hurried they might have trouble finding the trail up the other side of the canyon. All of a sudden his bare legs felt cold.

Now he gave quick instructions. "We'll use our Levis the same way and help you down first," he said to Denny. "Huff and I will hang onto you while you get over the edge. I'll come down last."

Denny eased himself down into the chimney, holding to Joe's right hand and Huff's left. He found a place to brace one foot on the big rock slab and pushed the other against the face of the chimney.

"Now let go our hands and grab the Levis," Joe ordered. "Huff and I will hold onto them tight so you can put all the weight you need to on them while you're sliding down to the ledge."

Denny did as he was told, but suddenly his foothold on the slab of rock gave way. There was a sickening grinding noise, a second of silence, and then a crash. The piece of rock he had been pushing against had broken loose. It must have been ready to fall, and Denny's weight was all that was needed to tear it loose. With a cry of fear, Denny found himself dangling from the Levis. There was nothing but space where his foot had found a resting place only a moment before.

"Are you all right, Denny?" Joe called in a voice filled with terror. He felt Denny's full weight on the Levis, and he knew he had to hold on with all his strength.

"Pull me up, quick," Denny choked out. "There's no place for my feet."

Bracing themselves as well as they could, Joe and Huff heaved backward on the Levis. In a few moments Denny's struggling figure lay on the floor of the cave in front of them.

For once Denny was frightened into silence. He was pale and trembling. Nobody spoke. As the excitement began to wear off, Joe and Huff felt weak, as if their muscles were made of soft rubber.

"Joe, what are we going to do?" Denny said at last. "I'm afraid some more rock will break off if I try to go down again."

Joe crawled to the edge and looked down the chimney. Since the sun had gone down, there were no sharp shadows to show him all the projections in the rock. The piece that had broken off had been a big one. He was not sure that even his long legs could reach clear across the chimney now. Probably he himself could not get down without a rope. Maybe they could tie all three pairs of Levis together and make a rope long enough to get them all down safely. On second thought, he decided that the seams at the crotch would surely split if weight were put on them. He thought of hitching all their belts together, but his was badly worn around the buckle and he was afraid that it would not hold their weight.

"Joe, get away from the edge," Denny said in a shaky voice. "It makes me kind of sick just to see you there. I'm scared."

"We have to think of something," Huff said.

Joe took the flashlight, stood up, and shot the beam all around the cave. Maybe he would see something that would give him an idea. For a moment he had a wild hope that he might find one of the ladders the Indians had used to reach the second stories of their houses. But not a one was in sight. Probably the cowboys who had used the cave had burned any ladders they found for firewood.

Now he had another idea. He picked up some rocks from the rubble and dropped them down the chimney. If he could pile a heap of stones on the ledge, they might be able to scramble down them to safety. But the ledge was too narrow, and the rocks bounded off into space.

Joe realized that he could not even see the ledge clearly now. Dusk was growing deeper. The two younger boys watched him in silence as he tried out one idea after another.

"Joe," Huff said finally, "I'm getting cold. Can I put

my pants on?"

"You better. I'm cold, too," Joe answered. "It's going to get a lot colder before morning, and it looks like we're stuck. I guess we'll have to spend the night here."

CHAPTER 9   In a Canyon, In a Cavern

"I bet Mom's going to have a fit," Huff said. "It would be just like her to believe that the rangers wait till fall to look for people who get lost."

"The rangers will hunt for us all night, and when they find us they'll scalp us alive," Joe added.

"They'll never find us," Denny said mournfully. "They don't even know this place is here."

"We can yell—or something. Unless you've lost your voice," Huff snapped crossly.

"It would be better to build a fire," Joe said. "I've still got some matches left from the campfire this morning. We'll build it right here where they can see it from across the canyon."

"Let's find some sticks," Denny said.

"Maybe we can make smoke signals," Huff suggested. "Like the Indians used to do."

"They couldn't see smoke. It's getting dark. But they could see the flickering of a fire that's not supposed to be up on the cliff anyway," Joe answered. "First we'll have to find wood."

The three of them went with the flashlight back into the cave.

"Look, there's a beam sticking out of this house. We can easy break it off," said Denny.

Joe was about to agree. Then he remembered how tourists were warned against touching anything in the cliff dwellings. That very beam might be of great value to the scientists.

"No," Joe said. "We can't burn that."

"Well, what else is there that we can burn?" Denny asked.

"Maybe nothing. Let's look a little more. All we can do is look. If we can't find anything, we'll use the flashlight as long as it lasts."

"I can flash SOS in Morse code," Huff said more hopefully. "I learned the whole code in the short wave at school."

By now the boys had walked along the whole length of the cave, beyond the house where they had found the two clay pots.

"Joe! Shoot your light over that way. I think I see something," Denny cried.

Following Denny's direction, Joe swept the light across the cave floor. Denny reached down and grabbed something.

"Look. A coffee pot. And here's a frying pan. That cowboy cooked here—this must have been where he had his fire."

Among charred bits of wood lay something that looked like a long thin stick. But when Joe kicked it, he found it was made of metal. "Looks like the cowboy's cooking bar," he said. He knew that cowboys out on the range often rigged up an iron rod across two Y-shaped sticks and hung their cooking pots on it over the fire. Maybe a couple of the sticks would still be lying around. He looked but he did not see them.

"A cooking bar and nothing to cook," Denny said disconsolately. "Gee, I'm hungry. Is there any chocolate left?"

"A little bit," Huff answered.

"We'll divide it in a minute," Joe said. "But first let's see if we can find enough wood for a fire."

Joe flashed the light around and found a small pile of juniper branches which the cowboy had probably brought in for kindling, because they burned so well. Near them were a couple of beams he might have torn out of a house to use, too.

"We'll take the sticks," Joe decided. "But we better leave the poles where they are. They might be genuine old-time beams."

They picked up the wood, and Huff also took the rusted iron rod and idly dragged it along back to the opening of the cave.

"Let's wait till it's pitch dark before we light the fire," Joe said. "We haven't got enough wood to last very long, and we want to be sure the rangers have got excited enough to start looking."

"Maybe you want to start yelling now," Denny said slyly to Huff. He was beginning to recover his natural good spirits. "You can yell while Joe and I divide up the chocolate."

"No harm to try," Joe said. "I expect they'll yell as they come along, though."

"What'll I holler?" Huff asked. "If I call 'Help!' they'll probably think we're hurt or dying or something."

"Can you yodel?" Denny said.

"Yeah," Huff answered, and unexpectedly he let out a professional-sounding imitation of a Swiss mountaineer. For a moment the two others stood in silent admiration of the feat, but only for a moment. A clear yodel came back from across the canyon.

"They're coming!" Huff exclaimed. He let out another earsplitting falsetto yawp. Again there was an answering yodel.

"Shucks," Joe said. "Let me show you something." Thrusting out his jaw he gave a special shrill whistle he had worked long in perfecting. In a moment they heard an identical sound in answer.

"Nuts," Huff said. "Nothing but an echo. But it's the best one I ever heard."

In front of the flashlight they divided up the last of the bittersweet chocolate. There was a handful of raisins left in the box, too.

"We're not sure how long we'll have to stay here," Joe said. "Let's just eat half of what we have now. The same with the water—if we have any left at all."

Denny had used all of his, and Huff's canteen was nearly empty. Joe had only about a cupful. "One mouthful apiece," Joe said. "That's all right now."

"Joe, do you mean we may be stuck here a long time and die of thirst or something?" Denny said.

"We're not going to die, but we can't be sure how long we'll be stuck up here. Till tomorrow morning, probably. The rangers would have a tough time getting us out of here tonight. I'd a lot rather stay till it's daylight and I can see what I'm doing. Wouldn't you?"

"But it will get cold," Denny said. He remembered how glad he had been to have his blankets the night before.

"Sure, but at least we'll be all in one piece," Joe answered.

"Don't you think we can start the fire now?" Huff asked. "That would warm us up a little, and it's dark as pitch."

"I think we better wait till we see flashlights down in the canyon," Joe said. "They are perfectly certain to come looking for us up the canyon, because Grandpa saw us going that way. Let's lay the fire, ready to start. And you two keep away from the edge. If you stubbed a toe it would be too bad for you."

Joe took out his knife and cut some shavings off one of

the sticks, so the fire would kindle easily when he lighted it. Then he piled it up, right on the far edge of the cave floor, so it would be most easily seen. Joe worked rapidly. He was worried about the flashlight now. Its batteries would wear out soon.

"Okay, you guys sit down. Huff over there, Denny on this side. And don't get up and wander around in the dark. It's dangerous." Then Joe took the flashlight from Denny. "We got to turn this off." Just as he was about to press the button, he saw in the beam of light the end of the iron rod Huff had picked up.

"The Rocking O!" he burst out.

"What you talking about?" Huff asked.

"Denny, look at that. It's a Rocking O branding iron. That came from our ranch."

"What's it doing up here?" Huff asked.

"Maybe Grandpa was here and left it," Joe said. "Or maybe one of the other cowboys from our ranch. In the old days they ran cattle here all the time."

"Let me see it," Huff said. He took the iron and examined the part of it that made the brand. "How do you get Rocking O out of this?"

Joe took it back and pressed it into the dusty cave floor.

When he pulled it up, it left a faint impression. "This curved line is the rocker," he explained. "And the circle is the O, of course. Now settle down because I'm going to douse the glim."

He turned the flashlight off and squatted down as close to the edge of the cave as he dared, so he could keep an eye out for any lights in the canyon.

All three of them sat in silence for some time. Each was thinking how chilly he was getting and how hungry he was and wondering how soon they would see the lights of rescuers. Suddenly, splitting through the silence, came the weird yelp of a coyote somewhere on the mesa high above them.

"What's that?" Huff asked in a whisper.

"Just a coyote," Joe answered. "I've heard them all my life, but they still give me shivers up and down my spine. One of those fellows can make himself sound like a half dozen, too. Somehow or other they seem to be able to throw their voices as a ventriloquist does."

As the coyote yowled again, and then again, Huff said, "It gives you the creeps, but at least it can't bother us down here."

"Coyotes don't ever bother people anyway," Denny said.

Again they fell silent, but not for long. A sharp high scream of agony and terror rose up from the canyon slope not far below them. Huff did not ask questions this time. He reached over and clutched Joe's leg. The scream sounded like a child or woman in great pain.

Joe sensed the fear in Huff's motion and wanted to re-assure him. "Sounds like a bobcat or something has just killed a rabbit," he said. "You'd never think a rabbit could make an awful noise like that, but when they're scared they do."

Huff's teeth were chattering, partly from fear of the mysterious sounds in the night and partly from the chilly air. He hated to seem like a sissy so he tried to keep quiet. But he kept thinking of the shirt that was in that Indian pot. If he just had it on, he might be a little warmer. At last his chill got the better of his pride, and he blurted out,

"Hey, let's match pennies to see who gets to put on that old shirt that's stuffed in the Indian pot. I'm pretty near freezing."

"You two flip for it," Joe said. "I'm all right." But he shivered as he said it.

"I'll trade you my chance at it for a square of your chocolate," Denny said.

"It's a deal," Huff replied. "Can we turn on the light for a minute, Joe?"

"Okay, you hold it and I'll get the shirt out," Joe answered. Chilly and worried though he was, Joe felt a kind of responsibility for the two pieces of ancient Indian pottery. Nothing must happen to them. Carefully he dug the shirt out of the large jar and tossed it over to Huff. The shirt was very big, and Huff put it on right over his baggy gray sweater. The shirt tails were long, so they hung nearly to his knees. At any other time, Joe and Denny would have laughed.

"That's better," Huff said. "Boy, when I think of my jacket at home—"

"Hurry up and sit down," Joe said. "I'm going to turn off the light."

Still there were no signs of searchers in the canyon below.

"I wonder what time it is," Denny said.

"I don't know. Maybe eleven—twelve—one. Anyway, it'll be a long time before the sun comes up. But it can't be too late. I figure they wouldn't have started out looking for us until maybe ten o'clock. Grandpa wouldn't start asking for help until dark. That would be about half-past nine. Say they started down the trail about ten, it would take them a good two hours at night to get anywhere near this place. And they might look for us up the left-hand fork of the canyon first."

"Can't we start the fire now, Joe?" Denny asked. "It's getting colder all the time."

"I'll tell you what," Joe answered slowly. "Let's take turns counting off seconds until a half hour is up. Then if we don't see any lights down below, we'll start the fire going anyway."

"One-double-and, two-double-and, three-double-and," Denny started, and when he finished off his minute, Huff counted. But after they had gone around three times, Denny complained, "This is no fun. Let's sing or something."

"In a canyon, in a cavern, excavating for some pots," Joe sang to the tune of *Clementine*. "Lived a Grogan in a hogan...."

They fooled a while longer making up verses like this, and as they sang, Huff's curious fingers discovered a pocket in the shirt, and something in the pocket. He pulled it out. It felt like a piece of paper folded up. He was just about to lean over and put it on the kindling for the fire when he had a second thought. It might be fun to see what the paper was.

"Joe, lend me the flashlight for a minute," Huff said. "I found a piece of paper folded up in the pocket of this shirt."

"Let's save the flashlight. I guess we can start the fire now. Wait till it blazes up, and then look at the paper," Joe answered.

He scratched a wooden match on the seat of his Levis and lit the shavings. Soon he had a small fire going. Denny wanted to throw on some more wood, but Joe would not let him.

"If anybody's looking for us, he'll see a small fire as easily as he'll see a big one," he said. "We have to save our wood."

For a minute Huff rubbed his hands near the flame, trying to get some warmth. Then he took the folded paper from the shirt pocket and squinted at it closely in the flickering light.

"It's old-fashioned writing. I can't read it," Huff said. "Want to look at it, Joe?"

Denny craned his neck to see, but gave up quickly when he saw the small, difficult hand.

Joe had trouble, too, in the firelight. He turned the flashlight on the paper and studied it for some time. At last he looked up and said,

"Wait till Grandpa sees this!"

CHAPTER 10   The Branding Iron

"What does it say?" Denny reached out his hand. "Let's see."

"Be careful, you'll tear it!" Joe cautioned him. "Wow, have we got something here!" Joe scrambled to his feet, full of excitement. But before he could explain what he meant, he stopped short and pointed down into the canyon. "Lights!"

"Where?" Huff jumped up and so did Denny. They crowded close to Joe so they could look through the narrow cave opening.

"Watch out! You nearly pushed me off the cliff," Joe cried.

"Can they see the fire?" Denny yelled.

"Maybe if I use the flashlight I can find out," Huff said. "I'll flash them a message in Morse code."

"Be still," Joe said. "Let's see if they yell."

The boys stared in silence in the direction in which Joe had seen the light. It had disappeared.

"Are you sure you saw anything, Joe?" Denny asked fearfully. "Maybe they've turned back."

"Maybe they're listening for us the same as we're listening for them," Huff suggested. "Let me try the flashlight, Joe."

"Try your yodel first," said Joe. "That won't wear out so soon."

Huff sang out the high sliding notes of his call. The echo came back quickly, and the three boys stiffened up, standing as near the cliff edge as they dared, waiting for any other sound that might come out of the night.

"I think I heard something!" Denny said in a suddenly loud stage whisper.

"Shh!" Joe and Huff warned him at the same time.

"Try it again, Huff," Joe ordered. "This time, Denny, you keep quiet so we can all be sure."

After Huff's call, there came a tiny, distant sound that might have been "Hel-l-l-o!"

Again Joe nudged Huff, and the same sound came in answer from down the canyon. This time a flash of light showed, too.

"They heard us!" Denny burst out, and he impulsively picked up a whole bunch of sticks and dropped them on the fire.

"Who told you to do that, Denny?" Joe said almost angrily. "It's still a long time till morning, and we're not off this ledge yet." He reached in and snatched from the fire as many of the sticks as he could without burning himself.

"Don't be so bossy," Denny protested.

Joe laughed. "I don't want to be a pain in the neck, but somebody around here has to think twice. When we're out of this mess, you can do whatever you feel like. But right now, no monkey business."

"Okay, okay then. Keep up that yelling, Huff," Denny said.

The light below kept appearing and disappearing, but gradually it came in the direction of their cave. The shouts were clearer now— "Hello—hello." Then, "Are you all right?"

Now Joe answered in his deep voice. "We're all right. Keep coming."

"Did you bring any food?" Denny chimed in.

"Wha-a-a-t?"

"Foo-oo-d!" Denny yelled.

Clear and bell-like came from the bottom of the canyon, "Baloney!"

Huff poked Joe and said, "Do you think they brought cheese, too?"

Any other time Joe might have laughed, but he could guess how angry the rangers must be at having to spend half the night scouring the canyons for three kids that did not have sense enough to come home for dinner. He only hoped that when he told them about the two pots they would calm down a little.

Before long, the boys could see three flashlights, and soon the rescuers were at the foot of the cliff below the cave. They and the boys could talk back and forth without any trouble. Joe explained that a big chunk of rock had broken off in the chimney so they could not get down, and before the rangers could interrupt he said they had found a hidden cliff dwelling and two perfect pots.

"Wonders never cease," said a sour voice from below, and Joe knew it belonged to Mr. Price, the ranger who had run them in for keeping a skull in the refrigerator.

"No fooling," Denny volunteered, "we made a real discovery."

"It better be good," Mr. Price shouted back. "Can't you three stay out of trouble?"

The rangers' lights had been playing over the face of the cliff. But Joe said, "I don't think there's any way to get us down tonight. Another piece of rock might break off. We can stay here all right till morning."

"*We'll* decide that," said Mr. Price. "First we'll have a look around."

The flashlights cast weird streaks of light over the rock curtain that closed in the cave. The rangers could see where the fresh break in the rock was, and fragments of it lay around their feet. The large chunk that had come loose lay far down the mountain side. There clearly was no way into the cave except the one which the boys had followed earlier.

"It seems to be safe up to the foot of the chimney," Price called to the others. "I'm going up there. Those kids are strong enough to get me on up with my rope."

Soon Price was on the ledge giving instructions to the boys above him. "I'll swing this coil of rope up to you. Catch it and then I'll tell you what to do next." With the coil in his right hand, he swung it from low down at his side, straight up over his head, and let go.

The rope sailed up into the dark, but not far enough for any of the boys to catch it. Down it came, slipping past Price and disappearing into the dark below him. The other rangers spotted it with their flashlights, and one of them scrambled up to the ledge with it.

Joe called over, "Wait a minute. We can let our belts down for the rope. That'll be a lot easier." Quickly the three of them hitched their belts together, and Joe dangled them over the cliff. In a minute he had the coil of rope in his hands and waited for further instructions from the rangers.

"Have you got a place there, back from the edge, where you can get a good solid brace with your feet?" Price called up.

"There's a caved-in kiva right close," Joe answered him.

"Couldn't be better," Price called back. "You—the tall one—you put one end of the rope around your waist. Do you know how to tie a bowline with a big loop?"

The boys shook their heads.

"All right. Send the end of the rope down and I'll tie it." Working in the dark, Price made a loop that was big enough to go over Joe's head and around his waist, but firm so that it would not slip in and tighten around his waist. "Okay, haul it up. Now you—what's your name?"

"Joe."

"You, Joe, climb down into that kiva, put the loop around your waist and face toward the edge of the cave. Then sit down. I want you to brace yourself with your legs at about a forty-five degree angle against the side of the kiva. That way I can come up the rope easily without putting any great strain on you. Now you other two kids stand aside, and if I need you to do anything I'll call."

When Joe was all set in the bottom of the kiva, the other two rangers took positions on either side so that their flashlights shone on the chimney through which Price had to scramble.

"Coming up!" Price called. Then he actually began walking up the face of the rock, holding his entire weight with his hands on the rope. The two boys saw him reach the edge of the cave with his body sticking out almost parallel to the floor. Then by pulling on the rope hand over hand, he drew himself upright and walked across the cave to the kiva.

"Joe, can you hold it while the others come up?" he asked.

"Nothing to it," Joe replied. "Tell them to come

right ahead."

Soon the other rangers were in the cave. Before they had a chance to tell the boys what they thought of them, Denny wanted to know if they had brought any food or water.

All except Price laughed. One of the men handed over a canteen and took some ham and cheese sandwiches from a knapsack on his back. Just as Joe thought Price was about to launch into a lecture, he turned the beam of his flashlight over toward the pots he had found.

"Look at those, Mr. Price. Aren't they beauties? I found them this afternoon. There may be more here."

"We saved all the beams, too," Denny said.

"Beans?" Price said.

"No, beams," Huff answered. "Denny means we didn't burn anything except some brushwood a cowboy had left here a long time ago. We were careful not to spoil any Indian things."

"What do you mean cowboy? How could a cowboy ever get in here?"

Joe had wondered the same thing during the long wait in the darkness, and he had figured out a theory. There must have been an easy entrance to the cave in the days when cowboys came here pot-hunting. First of all, he was sure the rock curtain had fallen after their particular cowboy left. The way in was so hard, for one thing, but also the cowboy fire was in a place where nobody in his right mind would have built it. The smoke from it would have filled the whole cave. So it stood to reason that the far end of the cave had been exposed to the air, not curtained by the rock when the cowboy used it.

"How are you going to get the pots down from here?" Denny asked.

"We'll worry about that later. They are as safe here as they would be in a bank. But you kids are getting out right now."

The ranger called Doc had been giving his attention to the pots. "Price, take a look at these things," he said. "They are as fine as anything we have in the museum." All three rangers were enthusiastic over the find, and the boys could see that Price had forgotten about the bawling out he planned to give them—for the moment at least.

"Bim," Price said to the third ranger, "do you mind rapelling down the rock? I need a good stout pole three or four feet long to use as an anchor for the last man out. There are some small trees right below and a little over to the right."

"Sure," said the man called Bim. And, while Price took Joe's place as anchor man in the kiva, Bim made deft turns of the rope around his body and then around one thigh, without tying any knots. Then he calmly turned around and walked backward down the face of the cliff, letting the rope which held him slip through his hands a little at a time. In almost no time at all he was at the bottom.

"Neat!" Denny exclaimed. "How did he do that? I want to try it."

"Not tonight, you don't," Mr. Price called up from the kiva. "That's only for experienced mountaineers. We'll let you kids down a safer way."

Soon the sound of Bim's hatchet reached the cave, and then he called, telling them to give a pull on the rope. A piece of piñon pine trunk about as thick as Joe's arm came up at the end of it. Mr. Price deftly wedged it at the bottom of the kiva and tied the rope to it. Then he climbed out and began working on the free end of the rope.

In a few minutes he had made a knot with two big loops. Then he showed Joe how to use one loop as a seat and the other as a brace for his back.

"Now we're going to let you clear down to the bottom of the cliff, Joe," he said. "You just keep yourself away from the wall with your feet and hands if necessary. Doc will stay right here and help you over the edge. I'll pay out the rope from down in the kiva."

Joe looked out into the night and down the thirty feet of cliff wall that was dimly lighted by Bim's flashlight, and he did not feel the least bit comfortable. "Could you keep the light out of my eyes?" he called nervously to Bim.

"Don't worry about the light," Doc said. "I'll get you over the edge. You can't fall. Just be sure the rope is under your seat. It's all right to hold onto the rope where the loops meet in front of you. But you don't need to. I could let you down in this thing if you were out cold. Just relax."

Relaxing was the last thing Joe felt like doing, but he was determined to be game. "Okay," he said tensely, "here goes."

In another moment he was hanging over empty space. Then he realized that he was slowly being lowered to the ground. Now and then he gave a gentle shove with one foot or the other to keep from swinging around with his

back to the cliff, and before he knew it his feet were on solid ground.

"Nothing to it!" he shouted up to Denny and Huff. "It's like going down an elevator. Huff, you try it next." He climbed out of the knots and in a few minutes Huff and Denny had joined him.

Shortly afterward Doc and Mr. Price stood beside them. They had rapelled down.

"How're you going to get your rope?" Denny asked.

Doc was amused, but he explained they would leave it so they could have an easy way back into the cave when they returned for the pots. "But if I catch you kids running off and climbing back up here—"

"Oh, my gosh, I have to go back," Joe said. "My branding iron's in there."

"Your *what?*" Mr. Price groaned.

"What next?" Doc demanded.

"Nobody's going back in there tonight," Bim said, but the rangers insisted on knowing what Joe was talking about.

As they all stumbled along down the trail, Joe told the story of the branding iron. Toward the end of it, his voice grew slower and wearier. He, and the others, too, sud-

denly felt exhausted. But Huff had just enough energy
to ask,

"Say, Joe, what about that paper I found in the pocket
of this shirt?"

CHAPTER 11   Jalopy for Sale

Joe's eyes smarted with weariness, and the vibration of the station wagon made it difficult for him to read the old-fashioned writing on the paper. But that did not really matter because he knew every single word of it by heart now:

> *The stage from Durango is running different days now. Don't know when the stuff is coming. You better see me right away. This Ute don't savvy English. I already paid him but you give him a dollar.*
>
> *Swink*

Joe glanced up from the note toward Grandpa who was driving. All the others in the car were asleep—Denny between Joe and Grandpa, Mrs. Hansen and Huff in the seat behind. The excitement and uproar of their return from the cave were all over, and the only one who seemed fresh and wide-awake was Grandpa. Mrs. Hansen had been up all night worrying herself and the park officials. None of the boys had got a wink of sleep either. But when they had reached the campground just after dawn, Grandpa was crawling out of his bedroll. He had not let the hurly-burly bother him the least bit.

Now Grandpa looked at the back seat through the rear-vision mirror and saw that Mrs. Hansen was sound asleep. "You think you had your troubles with those rangers," he said softly to Joe. "You should have seen what I had with *her* last night. She wanted me to wait up with her in the station wagon over by Balcony House. I couldn't see what good that would do anybody. It's a lucky thing I got my beauty rest. She was in such a bing-bang hurry to leave here this morning, and somebody has to be wide enough awake to drive."

Joe grinned appreciatively and shifted his position to a more comfortable one. The station wagon was making frequent sharp turns on the downhill road and Denny's limp form had gradually slipped over against him, pushing him against the door.

"I sure hate to leave," he said. "I think the rangers would have let us go back to the cave, and I bet there's a chance Bellyache Bill is cached away in the place somewhere. We didn't have a chance to look in nearly all the rooms."

"Don't be too sure," Grandpa answered. "You don't even know that the pots you found were mine. The branding iron might have been the one that was taken from me, I'll grant you, but it wasn't the only Rocking O iron in the world."

Joe shook his head and again went over the story he had been building up in his mind. The rustler had surprised Grandpa in Soda Canyon. Then he had unloaded the pack horses at the cave farther up the canyon—the cave the boys had discovered—which was the rustler's camp and hide-out. There he used Grandpa's branding iron for a cooking bar. Then a Ute Indian brought the message to him from Swink. Swink was in cahoots with the rustler who was part of the gang that robbed stagecoaches. The rustler must have turned the stolen horses over to the Ute, or to someone else in the gang, who sold them in Santa Fe or some other place where they would not be recognized. Then the rustler changed his shirt and socks, used the two pots as a storage cupboard, and lit out on his own horse with as light a pack as possible. He expected to return, but obviously he never did. Maybe he was even the man who was murdered in Swink's store. Maybe they had his skull with them in the car right now.

Grandpa broke into Joe's speculations. "If the mummy is in that cave you discovered, the rangers will find it in a hurry."

"But *I* want to find it," Joe said emphatically. "Now I can't even look for it. I'll probably never get back to the park."

Grandpa took his eyes off the road just long enough to glance sidewise at Joe whose weary face showed his intense feeling of being trapped. "Take it easy, Joe," he said. "There's a lot of the summer still ahead. I've got a notion something will work out. I'm not so sure my mummy and pots are still in that cave. How do you know the rustler didn't take them to the store in Canary City? He could have made himself some quick cash by selling them to Swink."

Joe had been figuring so hard on his own theory that he had forgotten all about the burned-out store. Suddenly Grandpa's line of thought gave him new hope and excitement. "Why didn't I think of that before!" he exclaimed. "That's just what he would have done." Then a discouraging idea crossed his mind. "One thing is sure. If the mummy was in the old store, there's nothing left of him now. He could never have lasted through that fire and all."

"One trouble with people nowadays is they are always in a hurry and jumping to conclusions," Grandpa said. "Take last night, for instance. Everybody seemed to think the world had come to an end when three kids didn't turn up for chuck. You'd think a body would starve to death missing a meal. Many's the time when I was your age I missed more than one meal and slept out without a bedroll. I had a hunch you and Denny knew enough about this country so you'd make out all right. But she, there, gave up hope and practically made your funeral arrangements."

Joe felt a sense of gratitude. He appreciated the fact that Grandpa was paying him a compliment. The old man considered Joe man enough to live the rough-and-ready life he had known sixty years ago. Joe began to relax, and in a short while the steady motion of the car put him to sleep.

The next thing he knew, Grandpa was ordering the garageman in Mancos to fill up the gas tank. Denny woke up with a start at the same time. He sat up straight and looked out the window.

"Where are we?" he demanded. "Let's get out and have a soda."

Outside in front of the vending machine at the garage, he reached in his pocket, then turned to Joe in dismay. "Hey, lend me a dime. All I've got is this phony fifty-cent piece."

"Here's one," Huff said.

With soda bottles to their mouths, the boys wandered toward a row of secondhand cars that were for sale. While the garageman checked the oil and put distilled water in the batteries of the station wagon, they gravitated as if by common agreement to the jalopy that was the oldest of the used cars. It was an old Ford coupe, knocked down, with no fenders and only a seat for the driver. Joe opened the rusty old hood and peeked at the engine while the others crowded around him.

"Boy, oh boy, what couldn't we do with that!" Denny said.

"What's so hot about it?" Huff asked.

"Look," Joe said. "It's got a strong chassis and it could take an awful beating. The engine looks all right. We could get the old head milled to raise the compression ratio, put on Clark headers and an Alquist intake manifold and dual carbs. Maybe we could even raise enough money to overbore the cylinders and put in some hot cams."

"Come again?" Huff said.

"Joe, couldn't we put in an aluminum fly wheel and stroke the shaft?" Denny said excitedly.

"We could," Joe said, "if the moon was made of green cheese. We don't have the money to do something like that, and besides I won't be able to get a driver's license for a while yet."

"You'll be old enough to get a license next month," Denny said. "And I'm going over to dig some more at the old store. I bet that gang hid the loot from stagecoach robberies at Swink's place."

"For once you may have a halfway sensible idea," Joe said. "The gang that held up the Durango stage must have had some place to cache their stuff, and the note showed that Swink was in with them. Some of the junk might still be there."

As the boys reluctantly piled back into the station wagon, Denny asked the garageman how much the old Ford cost.

"I've been asking fifty for the last three months," the man said. "But I'd take less to get rid of it. What's the matter—aren't you fellows satisfied with this station wagon?"

"Harold," Mrs. Hansen said, as Huff took the pop bottles back to the vending machine, "hurry. I want to get back to the ranch so that we can all have a real bath."

"I was willing to take a shower at Mesa Verde, but up there you said we had to hurry to get away," Huff answered.

"Come on, don't argue, Harold."

Grandpa came out of the garage office. "I just phoned the ranch, Mrs. Hansen," he said. "Lunch will be ready, and you and Huff and your husband are invited. I figured you wouldn't care too much about cooking when you get home."

Before Mrs. Hansen could answer, the garageman stuck his head up to the car window and said to Joe, "If you're really serious about that jalopy, guess I can let you have it for thirty-five."

"We're serious, all right, don't you worry about that. But we have to get the loot from a stagecoach first," Denny answered.

CHAPTER 12   Hardware—and Some Cash

"Hey, Huff!" Joe and Denny shouted over the noise of the creek and the rattle of the boards under their feet as they ran across the swinging bridge toward the Hansens' cabin.

Huff heard the racket and came outside to meet them.

"Did you hear?" Denny began.

"Of course, he didn't," Joe said. "We just heard it ourselves."

"Heard what?" Huff wanted to know.

"The hermit's dead!" Denny said. "Now we can go up there and dig again, I bet. Ask your ma if it's all right, Huff."

"What happened?"

"The state cops were just here and told Grandpa," Joe said. And then he explained. Three days ago somebody had found the old hermit's body up above timberline where he had been prospecting. Apparently he had died of heart failure. Whoever was supposed to do such things had gone through his shack to see if he left any property or a will. There was nothing. "Fibber says that anything we find in the old store now is ours without any argument —even a million dollars!" Denny added. "Let's get going."

"Joe, have you finished all of your chores yet?" Huff asked.

"I'm almost through," Joe said. "Mom will let me go after I've helped her with lunch."

Just then Mrs. Cutler beat the big iron triangle gong that hung outside the ranch house door. That meant lunch was ready.

"Come on, Denny, you might as well eat here again," Joe said. "You can do the dishes, while I get a pick and shovel and look up some screen or something to use for a sieve. Huff, you be ready."

"I'd rather eat home, I guess," Denny said.

"And lose your chance for that million dollars?" Joe remarked. "I'd do the dishes if I were you."

Denny saw he was in a trap and went to lunch without much enthusiasm.

By the time they reached the site of the old store, the three boys had worked out a plan for digging. They decided to be scientific, the way the experts at Mesa Verde were. They would make an exploratory trench through the rubble, starting at the place where they had found the meat block and the skull, then working toward the back of the store, which was against the hillside. As they dug, they would face the hillside and throw the stones to the left beyond the boundaries of the old store. When they had dirt to shovel out, they would fill a bucket and sift it on top of the new stone pile. Grandpa had given them an old piece of screen to use for this.

Except for finding a few more bones from the murdered man, the digging was dull business. It was hard work to lift the stones and throw them to one side, and nothing interesting appeared on the screen as they shook it back and forth to sift the earth. Then suddenly Denny let out a whoop.

"I told you we'd get rich. I told you we'd get our jalopy. Look at this!"

A dirt-covered coin appeared in the shovelful of earth and charred wood he dug up. He filled the bucket, ran over, and poured the earth out on the screen while Joe

and Huff shook it back and forth. Another coin turned up as they shook.

"Two quarters!" Denny shouted. "I'll fill another bucket."

There was nothing in the next or the next, but the fourth and fifth buckets yielded three more quarters and a fifty-cent piece. By the time they were so tired they had to rest, they had sifted out five dollars and twenty-five cents worth of quarters and half dollars. They had struck the hard-packed earth that had been the floor of the store, so now they had to pull away more stones in order to find more earth to sift.

"I bet we're just beginning to get the loot from the stagecoach robberies!" Denny said, looking dreamily off into the distance, as if he saw the jalopy there waiting for him.

"I bet you no such thing," Joe said. "It looks to me like we have just dug at the place where old Swink kept money in a drawer for making change. I'll be surprised if there's much more there. Remember, Grandpa said Swink had gone to the bank to deposit his money when the fire broke out."

"What do you talk that way for?" said Denny crossly.

"You want the jalopy as much as I do."

"I expect there *are* a lot of interesting things to find here," Joe said. "But we won't know till we get the whole place dug down clean as a whistle. Come on, let's get back to work."

They had to pull away more stones now. Before long, Joe's pick pried up something hard and heavy that was not a rock. It was a miner's drill, all rusted and caked with earth. Around it he turned up other drills of various lengths.

"See, I told you we'd find something if we kept at it," Joe said. "Maybe we're in the store's hardware department."

In another half-hour of steady digging, they found several heads for hammers that miners used for drilling. There were some ordinary hammer heads, too, and heaps of rusted bolts and nuts.

"This stuff's no use," Denny said. "We can't even sell it for junk."

Then Huff came on a nest of old metal pans, one inside the other.

"Those were used for panning gold," Joe said. "I've seen them."

By now they had reached the stone wall, laid directly against the hillside, which had formed the back of the old store. Then Joe pulled away a rock, and instead of finding the stone wall behind as he expected, he discovered an empty space.

At first Joe started to call the others. Then he decided to explore a little further before he got them excited. Digging carefully so that the side walls of the trench would not give way, he broadened the end of the trench. As he did so, the opening in the wall grew larger. Joe reached in with his arm and found emptiness as far as he could reach.

"Hey, fellows! Here's a tunnel or something that goes back into the hill!" he called.

Scrambling over the rubble, Huff and Denny came to look and to stick their arms through.

"Boy! Have we found something! I bet the loot's all in there," Denny said. "I bet it's an old mine shaft that goes way into the mountain. There is sure to be plenty of room to store all kinds of loot."

"Whatever it is, we can't find out now," Joe said. "It will take hours to dig away the rocks and dirt here before we can get a hole big enough to crawl through. Look where the sun is. I expect the dinner gong has already rung. We'll have to come back again tomorrow and go on."

"Oh, come on, let's explore now," Denny protested. "It won't hurt anything if we're a little late for dinner this once."

"We'll be a lot late before we get into that tunnel, moving these rocks and things. It's slow work right here," Joe answered. "Besides, we haven't got flashlights so we have to stop."

Both the younger boys were irritated at having to stop, but on the way back across the meadow they began to speculate about the discoveries they would make in the tunnel when they finally got into it. And at least they had five dollars and a quarter in actual cash to show for their work.

Suddenly, thinking of that, Huff exclaimed, "You know what, I bet that money is worth more than we think it is. It's real old. And it's genuine money, not Confederate stuff like your fifty-cent piece, Denny."

"How much do you think we could get for it?" Denny asked.

"I don't know," Huff said, "but why couldn't we find

out as soon as we get home? Wouldn't your grandfather let us telephone the store in Durango, Joe? We could pay him for the call."

"Maybe," Joe said.

At the ranch house, Mrs. Cutler had dinner on the table when Joe and Denny arrived, and afterward Grandpa pointed out that the store would almost certainly be closed by this time.

"You can phone tomorrow," he promised. Then he asked the boys what else they found. Joe told him about the pans and hammers and nuts and bolts.

At the mention of the hardware, the old man's eyes began to wander around the cluttered walls of the sitting room as if he were recollecting something. He heaved himself out of his chair and went over to a faded photograph that hung between a wolf skin and a pair of large elk horns.

"See that?" he said pointing to the canvas-covered wagon in the picture. "I was driving a freighter just like this, helping to bring supplies into Canary City one time. A bunch of us were coming in from Santa Fe direction, and at one place we had to ford a river. My horses got spooked in the water, and the whole outfit turned over.

About everything in the wagon dumped out. The bottom of the river was pretty well paved with nuts and bolts and hardware like that. The stuff you found today reminded me of it. The place where we spilled was pretty deep, but the horses somehow got the wagon into shallower water and me with it, which was a good thing because I didn't know anything more about swimming than I did about flying.

"Some Navahos saw the pickle I was in, and they came around to watch the excitement. One way and another I managed to let them know about the stuff that had dumped out of the freighter. Before I knew it, those Navahos were out there with their heads down under water and their legs up in the air, behaving like ducks in a pond. I was surprised that desert Indians knew how to swim, but they sure did.

"They rescued just about all of the nuts and bolts, and when I gave them some of the nuts to make necklaces with, they waited around to do me and the rest of the wagon train another good turn. Across the river was a band of Utes that just happened by. I guess it must have been the Utes that spooked my horses in the first place. It didn't take a lot of studying on the situation to see that they weren't exactly friendly. They didn't want us to cross the river, because we were bringing in more stuff for the whites who were taking their land away. At that time, whites weren't moving into Navaho country much, and the Navahos were so pleased about the hardware I'd given them that they were ready to be our bodyguard. They didn't shoot off any guns or arrows or anything. They just swam their ponies across the river on either side of us and rode along for a while kind of careless-like, until the Utes got the point and vamoosed. I wonder if some of the nuts and bolts I brought in that wagon might be the ones you dug up today."

"Gee," said Denny. "We'll bring some back tomorrow so you can see."

Joe laughed. "Do you think they'd have Grandpa's fingerprints left on them after all these years?"

"Well, anyway, we found some money and a tunnel," Denny said unabashed. "And probably some loot from stagecoaches."

"What's this about a tunnel?" Grandpa asked.

The boys explained about the opening they had found at the rear of the old store.

"Oh, I know what you mean," Grandpa said. "Old

Swink had some kind of hole in the rock there at the back where he put meat to keep it cool. Don't get too excited. You won't find anything there but some ham bones and a beef rib or two."

CHAPTER 13 Loot?

When Huff told his father about the coins they had found in the ruins, Mr. Hansen was interested. He planned to drive into Durango in a couple of days, and he offered to take the boys with their money to the curio store then.

But two days was a long time to wait. By the middle of the morning they were restless. Grandpa said it was high time they taught Huff to ride a horse, and for an hour Joe and Denny gave him a lesson on the gentle old mare the Cutlers kept for tourists to use. After a trip or two at a walk up and down the lane in front of the Rocking O ranch house, Huff felt confident enough to put his horse into a trot. Joe showed him how cowboys took the rise-and-fall of a trot without getting jounced at every step, and Huff caught on quickly.

Afterward they went to the kitchen for a glass of milk,

and the restlessness returned. They wanted to know *now* whether their coins were valuable. But none of them was willing to make a long distance telephone call to the curio store in Durango. They had a firm conviction that the dealer would not give a straight, honest answer to a kid.

At last Mrs. Cutler said with a smile, "All right, I'll keep you from exploding on the spot. I'll call the store for you."

Huff had made a list of the coins and the dates on them. He felt pretty sure the dealer would ask for dates. With the quarters and half dollars in a pile on her desk, and the boys hovering close by, Mrs. Cutler put the call in. Presently she began to read off the dates. Then she said, "No, I don't know. I'll have to look." Taking a pencil, she made some notes on Huff's list. "I'll call you back," she finished.

"How much are they worth?" Denny asked.

"What are you going to look for?" Huff wanted to know.

"Hold your horses," Mrs. Cutler replied jovially. "Wait till I get Papa's magnifying glass. Now, Joe, you use the glass while I read off what the man said to look for. He said there might be little letters under the eagle on some of the coins, and that would make them more valuable. The letters show where the coin was minted, and some coins from some mints are valuable. The man told me that the ones that looked new were worth more than old worn ones."

Quickly the boys arranged the coins according to dates. Then Joe squinted through the magnifying glass looking for letters beneath the eagle on the back of each one. Several of the quarters were dated 1889, 1890, and 1891. None of these seemed to have any small letters on them. One that seemed to have been used a lot, however, had a tiny S on it, and on the other side was the date 1878.

"How much do you suppose that's worth? A hundred dollars?" Denny said.

"*She* doesn't know," Huff broke in. "She has to phone back."

Another quarter dated 1873 had S under the eagle. Two half dollars had none of the mysterious small letters, but one, dated 1878, showed what looked like a worn-down CC. Mrs. Cutler checked over the list and when it was complete, she phoned the dealer again.

"First," she said when she got him, "could you tell me what those little letters mean? I found some S's and some CC's."

As she listened to the reply, she wrote down San Francisco and Carson City. "Thank you," she said finally. "I'm sending my son in day after tomorrow. He'll bring the coins with him."

"How much?" Denny demanded.

Mrs. Cutler laughed and read down the list. They could get at least seventy-five cents for every one of their quarters. The 1873 quarter with S on it might be worth two dollars. The 1878 half dollar marked CC might be worth ten. Sight unseen, the dealer offered twenty dollars for the whole lot, and he said he might even be willing to pay twenty-five.

"How do you like that!" Denny cried. "That's almost enough to buy our jalopy! Let's go and dig up some more quick."

That afternoon, as soon as they could get there, they were back at work excavating the old store. Denny and Huff sifted what seemed like tons of earth, looking for more coins. But Joe enlarged the opening of the tunnel. In spite of what Grandpa had said about finding only meat bones, he had a secret hope that he might discover something valuable in there—maybe even Bellyache Bill.

When he had a hole large enough to squeeze through,

he called to the others, "Here I go. You guys wait outside." Flashlight in hand, he wiggled through the opening. "Hey, it's big!" he called. He shivered, because the air was chilly and damp and musty. "There's a mess of junk lying around. Do you want to come and look?"

"Did you find any loot?" Huff called, trying to imitate Denny's voice.

In another minute, all three, using flashlights, were poking around in the debris that littered the tunnel. Apparently miners had started to drive a shaft into the mountain here and then abandoned the effort after going through about twenty-five feet of solid rock.

A pile of what seemed once to have been canned food lay in one place. There were, indeed, the meat bones that Grandpa had said they would find. They were not charred, so apparently the fire had not spread all the way back into the tunnel.

As Joe surveyed the damp, shapeless heaps, he began to lose hope of finding Bellyache Bill, even if by some chance the mummy had been put into the tunnel. It would have decayed in this moisture, and it was clear that mountain rats living here would have destroyed anything that was left of it.

"Everything's rotted and rusted down to nothing," Denny said disgustedly.

Even Joe felt more and more disappointed as he looked around. Then his flashlight picked out an object far back in the tunnel. It seemed to be set into a recess in the solid rock.

Joe looked more carefully. What he found was a small safe. Once paint had covered the thick metal of it. Now rust bulged up under much of the paint, and it was a time before Joe noticed that the door of the safe was just slightly ajar.

Here might be a discovery worth the whole trouble of excavating—and many times over!

Even Joe, who was always practical, wondered if there might be stagecoach loot inside. He tried the door, but it would not budge a fraction of an inch. Long years ago rust had frozen the hinges.

"Denny, go out and get the pick! If there's any loot in this joint, I've found where it is and I need the pick," Joe called.

Denny moved fast—but not in the direction of the pick. "No fooling! What're you talking about?" he exclaimed.

"A guy doesn't have a safe unless he has something

special that he wants to keep safe in it, does he? Look at this."

"Well, let's crack it," Denny said.

"That's why I want you to get me the pick," Joe answered.

"Huff! Go get the pick," Denny shouted.

"I don't know where it is," Huff said.

"You're a big help," Joe grumbled, heading for the patch of light which was the opening of the tunnel. In a minute he was back.

"Give it here," Denny said excitedly.

"Hold the light and move out of the way," Joe answered as calmly as he could. His pride had kept him from showing more excitement than the younger boys up to now. But he had found something that looked much like a tremendous discovery. Now his pride had disappeared. "Get out of the way. Let me work on this."

Trying first the pointed end of the pick and then the flat end, he struggled to pry the safe door open. As he heaved, with the point in the crack, the whole safe shifted a bit, but the door did not budge.

"Get some stones. We'll wedge this thing in against the wall so it can't shift, and then I'll try forcing the door again," Joe ordered.

This time the two others ran with their flashlights to do as Joe told them. When they had chucked rocks in between the safe and the solid wall surrounding it, Joe again wedged the flat blade of the pick into the crack between the door and the side of the safe. Slowly, carefully he pulled on the pick handle. But the blade slipped loose and he tumbled over backward. He tried again, and again the pick slipped when he put pressure on it. The crack simply was not wide enough for him to get a good purchase.

"Let me try," Denny begged.

"Okay, go ahead and try, but we've got to get something with a thinner blade," Joe answered.

Denny made a big fuss about putting the blade into the narrow crack and then heaved backward with a resounding grunt. When the pick slipped, he fell with such a thud that Joe and Huff, in spite of their excitement about the safe, had to laugh.

"I know," Huff said. "Let's try some of those old drills." He scrambled out through the tunnel entrance and was soon back with a couple of the rusted old rock-drilling tools that they had unearthed the day before. He tried one after another on the edge of the safe door. All were too blunt for the job.

Joe reluctantly said, "I guess we'll just have to go home and see if Grandpa has some better safecracking tools."

CHAPTER 14   Mormon Gold

"Do you think these will do, Joe?" Grandpa asked. "They're a couple of wrecking bars I got when I pulled down the old barn."

Joe looked carefully at the tool the old man handed him. It was just about the size and shape of a cane with a curved handle, except that at both ends there were tapering blades. He ran his finger over the dull, rusty edge at the end of the long shank.

"Can we use the grindstone on these?" he asked. "They ought to be a lot thinner and sharper or they won't be any good."

"Oh, come on, Joe. Let's not fool around," Denny said impatiently. "These will do."

"They won't do if they won't go in that thin crack," Joe answered. He was as eager as the others to get back to the safe and get it opened, but he knew he could not use a thick instrument.

So, while Denny and Huff took turns pumping on the foot treadle of the old-fashioned grindstone, Joe thinned down the blades of the wrecking bars.

"If you get them any thinner I can shave with them," Grandpa said at last. "Then they'll be no good for prying. Come on. Hop in the pickup truck and I'll drive you over."

He threw in a couple of big hammers and a cold chisel, and they were off, through the wire gate in the pasture fence on the other side of the creek, then over the knobbly turf, right up to the old store.

Showing the way through the trench they had dug, the boys led Grandpa to the tunnel. Joe was delighted that his grandfather seemed just as excited as he was about the safe in the cave.

"I can't recall that anybody knew Swink's meat cellar was as big as this," Grandpa said. "But I guess we wouldn't have paid much attention anyway. I suppose it was reasonable for him to have a safe, too. Still it's a wonder somebody didn't come and get it out before now. I guess that hermit son of his was even crazier than we thought. Swink's wife was dead long before the fire, of course, and other folks had their minds on striking it rich by prospecting."

While Denny and Huff held the flashlights, Grandpa helped Joe wedge one of the bright blades into the crack in the safe door. "Now, Denny," the old man said, "you tap with that hammer all around the edge of the door. Maybe you can break loose some rust. But be careful not to bang too hard. You don't want to force the door shut."

Suddenly Joe looked up with dismay. If the safe door was open, it probably meant there was no valuable loot in it. And, of course, Swink had taken his own money to the bank. Joe started to speak and then thought better of it. He was still curious. When Denny finished tapping, Joe pressed slowly, firmly on the wrecking bar. Nothing happened, but at least the bar did not slip out of place. He pulled harder and harder, digging his heels into the uneven surface of the tunnel floor. Then there came a slight sagging feel in his hands and the door gave.

Inch by inch, Joe pried the stubborn door open. Denny and Huff thrust their flashlights at Grandpa and grabbed hold of the edge to pull with their hands. All together they forced it open far wide enough so that they could easily

peer inside.

Joe was surprised at how small the space in the safe was —its steel walls were very thick. A quick feeling of confusion and disappointment came over him. There was nothing visible inside but a small heap of disorderly papers. Above the heap he made out two small metal drawers. With difficulty he managed to wiggle them open. In one, there was nothing but a small bundle of business papers and a few letters. The other held a small cream-colored box that looked as if it was made of ivory.

"Let's see what's in the box," Denny said, reaching for it eagerly.

"Be careful," Huff warned. "You might break something."

Denny put the box on top of the safe and lifted off the lid. The yellow column of light from Huff's flashlight showed a lock of blond hair and a picture of a chubby young woman who was dressed in an old-fashioned dress with big puffed-out sleeves, a high neck line, and a very long skirt.

Grandpa said, "Probably Swink's wife." He lifted the photograph to examine it more carefully. Under it lay a gold chain which was attached to something that looked like a medal.

"This must be a decoration she hung around her neck," the old man guessed.

"Well, there's all your stagecoach loot, Denny," Huff said.

"Nuts," Denny answered. "Maybe there's something under the papers." He bent down and began pulling things out of the heap.

Meanwhile Joe fingered through the bundle of papers he had taken out of the drawer. "Here's some mining stock, Grandpa," he said. "Do you think it might be worth anything?"

Grandpa looked at it and snorted. "I know a fellow who papered his bedroom with that stuff. That's all it's good for."

Denny gave up pawing through the heap of papers in the safe. Huff began disconsolately playing the flashlight up and down and around the rough rock wall. Joe swung one leg over the safe door and rested his weight there wearily.

"Joe," Grandpa said sympathetically, "you're feeling the way prospectors do, ninety-nine times out of a hundred. You only strike it rich once in a long while when you dig in these mountains. Anyway, I want to take some of this junk home and look at it. I kind of enjoy being reminded of old times."

Joe poked a fistful of papers into one pocket and the small ivory box into another.

That night after dinner, Mrs. Cutler looked at the box. "My mother had one almost exactly like that when I was a girl," she said. "It was for keepsakes. I wonder whose hair this is. It's kept real well."

Huff looked at the photograph that still lay in the ivory box. Then he wandered about the sitting room, examining Grandpa's many old pictures. He fingered a bearskin that hung on the wall next to a faded brown photograph of a group of cowboys.

"I wish I had a wild animal skin for my room at home," he said, half to himself. "It would make it look more like a den."

Joe reached into the ivory box and picked up the medal on its chain. Holding it so the light would fall on its raised surface, he read out, " 'Holiness to the Lord.' "

Grandpa looked up quickly. "What's that you said, Joe?"

"This locket's got 'Holiness to the Lord' written on it,

that's all. Some sort of religious thing, I guess." Joe turned it over, then let out a long, low whistle. "Pure gold!" he exclaimed.

"It's probably brass," Huff put in. "You can't tell without testing."

"No, the words say 'Pure gold—ten dollars—eighteen-forty-nine!'" Joe answered.

"Holy smoke! Let me see that," Grandpa said. "I've got a notion what it is. Pass me my magnifying glass, Joe." He looked at the yellow disc. "Yes, sir, that's a Mormon ten-dollar gold piece."

"What do you mean Mormon?" Joe asked.

"Yep," Grandpa said. "When the Mormons moved out here, right next door in Utah, they kind of set up their own country for a while. They made all their own money. That was about the time of the big gold rush to California in '49, and the money they made was really pure gold, just like it says here. So people kept on using it for a long time after the Mormons got regular money from Uncle Sam. Later, the gold pieces became souvenirs. I used to see them hung on watch fobs when I was a kid. It looks like somebody rigged this one up into a necklace instead of using it for spending money."

"Gee, if this is a real coin, I bet it's worth more than all our others put together," Huff said.

"We found some loot after all," Denny chirped. "We'll all be rich."

CHAPTER 15

The Huffmobile

"The treat's on us," Joe announced as he held open the door of the Columbine Soft Drink Parlor to let his mother and grandfather in. Denny tried to squeeze past, but Joe held him by the scruff of the neck. Denny had to put on some manners, for this was a special occasion.

Denny and Huff wanted to sit at the soda fountain, but Joe shooed them into a booth. The party today had to be done in style, and sitting at the fountain seemed too easy and ordinary.

"You can order anything you want, Mom and Grandpa," Joe said.

"I want a giant jumbo chocolate milk shake," Denny announced.

"And a lot of other things, too, I expect," Joe said. "Didn't you hear me say company is supposed to order first?"

"I have to see the meenoo," said Grandpa.

The bustling young waitress explained there was no "meenoo." You had to read the signs around the shiny chromium soda fountain that was built in the shape of a horseshoe in the center of the large room.

"Torpedo," Grandpa read off. "What's a torpedo?"

Mrs. Cutler knew the answer. She visited the Columbine every time she came to Durango. "That's an outsize malted milk, so big and thick it'll sink you," she said.

"Malted milk!" Grandpa shuddered. "That stuff smells like nothing but cow feed. I'm not going to ruin my health and bankrupt these three millionaires for any such fodder as that. What's a giant jumbo black and white?"

Denny pointed to a quart-sized glass shaped like an ice cream cone. "It's that thing, full of vanilla ice cream, chocolate ice cream, and a lot of extra squirts of syrup, and fizzed up good with soda."

Grandpa shuddered again and read some more signs. "Ah! 'All the buttermilk you can drink for ten cents!' What's the trick in that?" he asked the waitress.

Smiling, she answered, "No trick at all, sir. It means just what it says. But you have to get to the door under your own power."

"Well, I'll be! I never had enough buttermilk in my life. Here goes," Grandpa said. "Buttermilk for me and for this lady, too. Isn't that right?"

"Sure," said Mrs. Cutler.

"Now, Huff, you've been quiet. It's your turn next," Joe said.

"What's that thing that Denny wanted to order?" Huff asked.

"It's the most famous thing in town," Denny broke in. "Everybody knows you're supposed to have a giant jumbo chocolate milk shake when you come to the Columbine. It's just quarts of milk shake so thick you have to eat it with a spoon."

"Okay," said Huff.

"Make it three," Joe said to the waitress.

While the soda jerk made grand and professional gestures at the fountain, Grandpa began to complain, "I tell you, kids, you must have been cheated. If that old crook who runs the curio store paid you two hundred and seventy-six dollars for your collection of old-fashioned money, it must have been worth three or four or maybe five times that much."

"Now, keep still, Papa," Mrs. Cutler said comfortably.

"You know we got the best bargain we could. I never saw the day when an old horse trader like you was beaten in a deal."

"We're satisfied," Joe added. He already had a pencil out and was doing arithmetic on a paper napkin. "Thirty-five dollars for the jalopy. Thirty for new parts. That's what we agreed on—if we got that much."

Last night, after they discovered they had the 1849 Mormon gold piece, there had been a long and heated discussion about what would happen to any money they got from the sale of the coins. The argument went on so long that Mr. Hansen came to the ranch house to look for Huff, and he was drawn into it, too. Huff had said first off that Joe and Denny should have their jalopy, even though he would not be around much to ride in it. After all, they were the ones who had invited him to go digging in the beginning, and they had let him keep all the rock specimens —and the skull.

"From this day on, the jalopy's name is going to be the Rocking O Huffmobile," Joe said.

Mrs. Cutler and Mr. Hansen had agreed that it was not unreasonable to spend thirty-five dollars for the old car. But Joe argued that they had to have at least thirty dollars for parts to get the jalopy going. The grownups finally agreed to this—on condition that everything else, if there was anything else, be divided evenly among the three boys and put into the bank for college.

Denny had wanted to spend all of his share right away, and he argued endlessly against going to college. But finally he gave in. If Huff could give away money toward a jalopy, he could give away money toward college.

Now Joe finished his figuring on the napkin. "This is it: we've each got seventy dollars and thirty-three and a third cents to put in the bank."

"I'll match you for your third of a cent," Denny said to Huff.

"Hold it, I forgot to take out for this treat," Joe said. "That will make it just seventy dollars each, and I'll throw in the extra dime."

The waitress began shuttling back and forth with quart-sized glasses of milk shake and the two quart bottles of buttermilk.

"First one through gets a second," Denny announced.

"The seconds are on you, then," Joe said. "If you can buy them with your phony fifty-cent piece."

"Nuts," Denny replied and began to work on his

milk shake.

Joe looked at the clock on the wall. "Mom, couldn't we go and get the jalopy this afternoon? It's only three o'clock."

"I'm sorry, Joe, you'll have to wait," Mrs. Cutler answered. "It's not fair to leave Mrs. Hansen at the ranch house too long. Maybe some guests have come and she won't know all the things to do to take care of them. It might take a long time to get the sale papers made out. Even if the jalopy runs, you haven't got license plates for it, so it will have to be towed behind the pickup truck, and that means slow driving. I have to fix dinner for the three people in cabin two—"

Joe suspected his mother was talking sense, although he hated anything that delayed buying the jalopy. "Then why can't we drop you at the ranch and let Grandpa take us to get it?"

"You need somebody with a driver's license to steer the jalopy," Grandpa said. "That's a law."

"I could ask my father to drive the pickup," Huff said, "only you know he's not feeling well today." He knew his mother would not be any use.

"I'll get my brother Buck," Denny said.

"No, it's just too complicated," Mrs. Cutler said firmly. "I'll go with you tomorrow afternoon for sure. I'll drive the pickup and Grandpa can come along to steer the jalopy home."

Suddenly an awful thought occurred to Joe. "Say! Maybe our car has been sold already. Grandpa, phone the garage right now. Please."

"I don't like hot phone booths," Grandpa said.

Doggone it, Joe thought, couldn't any grown person understand about getting your first car? But he said cheerily, "Aw, come on, we'll pay for the call."

"I've got about a half pint to go on this buttermilk," Grandpa said. "If I'm not foundered by then, I'll call the guy."

All three boys fidgeted and squirmed while the old man took his time with the last of his buttermilk. Then like a bodyguard they went with him to the back of the shop and hovered around the phone booth while he made the call. They could not hear everything he said, but in a few minutes he came out with a twinkle in his eye and a wide grin.

"Saved you some money," he said.

Joe's heart sank. "You mean our jalopy is gone?"

"No, I got it for thirty dollars instead of thirty-five. How's that suit you?"

As they walked out of the Columbine, Mrs. Cutler found herself next to Denny. "Well, are you happy?" she asked.

"Yep—except for one thing," Denny said.

"What in the world more can you have your heart set on?" Mrs. Cutler was usually not surprised at anything boys did or said. But it did seem to her that the jalopy plus the giant jumbo milk shake would do for one afternoon.

"I still want that skull," Denny answered a little mournfully. "And I had to go and let Joe talk me into saying that it was Huff's."

Mrs. Cutler could not help laughing. Then an idea came to her. "Denny, have you still got that mountain lion skin that your brother Buck gave you last winter when he shot it?"

"Sure—why?"

"Buck cured it pretty well, didn't he?"

"Oh, sure. He knows how to fix skins up good."

"Well, why don't you bring it over tonight and show it to Huff?"

"I don't know—it's just like the one in your sitting room, except it doesn't have any head on it."

"All the better," Mrs. Cutler said. "Don't forget now. You bring it over."

CHAPTER 16   Lion Skin Game

"What you got there?" Joe asked as Denny came into the ranch house sitting room with a large bundle in his arms.

"My lion skin."

"Did you lug that all the way over from your place?"

"No, I hitched a ride with Buck," Denny answered.

"What did you want to bring it over here for, anyway?" Joe asked. "I thought we were going to plan out about the jalopy."

"You wait till Huff gets here and then you'll see," Denny said. He had got the point of Mrs. Cutler's hint.

"Look," Joe said, pointing to several worn copies of a hot-rod magazine that he had brought from his room. "I never thought I'd ever get to use these, except for reading."

The two of them flopped down on the bearskin rug with the magazines, and just then Huff came in. Mrs. Cutler looked up expectantly from the table where she and Grandpa sat examining the old papers Joe had brought back from Swink's store.

"Hi," Huff said.

Joe and Denny nodded and kept on their discussion of plans for the jalopy. Huff tried to work up an interest in one of the copies of the magazine, but he soon put the magazine down. Automobiles were good for going places, and that was as far as he was interested in them.

Mrs. Cutler and Grandpa were talking back and forth about things that the old papers recalled. There were some letters about mining rights which brought names to Grandpa's mind, and he reminisced about one person and another who did not interest Huff at all. Altogether he felt left out, and he began to wander restlessly around the room, looking at Grandpa's trophies.

"What's this?" he asked of no one in particular when he saw the bundled-up mountain lion's skin on the floor by the door.

"My lion skin," Denny replied.

"No fooling! Let me see it," Huff demanded.

"All right. You can untie it and look at it."

While Huff spread out the big tawny piece of fur,

Denny watched him cannily. Mrs. Cutler, too, looked up and winked at Denny.

"This is neat!" Huff exclaimed. "Is it really your own?"

"Sure. My brother gave it to me and I can do anything I want with it. You don't see skins like that much any more. Mountain lions are getting scarcer—especially ones as big as that."

Huff stretched the tail clear out to gauge the animal's size.

"He measured nearly eight feet from his nose to the tip of his tail," Denny said. "I never expected Buck would give him to me, but he did."

Huff sat stroking the fur and examining the gradations in color. The under part of the belly was nearly white and so was the underside of the tail which ended in a pure black tip. "Gee, I'd give anything to have something like this for my den," he said.

"Too bad you haven't got a brother who goes hunting," Denny said, catching Mrs. Cutler's eye. Then he turned back to the magazines, leaving Huff to work up some more collector's enthusiasm. In a minute, Huff was draping the skin across the old sofa. Then he sat down and wrapped it around himself.

"I'd pretty near trade you all my mineral specimens for this," Huff finally said.

Denny just shook his head without looking up.

"I can just see it," Huff went on dreamily. "I'd hang it on my wall in front of my desk, and I'd put my skull on the desk right underneath it."

All this time Joe had been figuring out that Denny was up to something, and he saw that the remark about the skull had somehow caught Denny short.

"Do you mean to say your mother will let you keep the skull in your room after the way she carried on about it?" Joe asked.

Huff said nothing, but his face revealed that he knew his mother *would not* let him keep the skull where anybody could see it. She still would not allow him to have it inside their cabin here. It had to stay wrapped up in a carton on the cabin porch.

"Do you think she'd let you keep a lion skin hanging on the wall?" Denny asked.

"I'm sure she'd do that," Mrs. Cutler put in. "She's often said how pretty she thought some of our skins are."

"I'll tell you what, Huff. I'll do you a favor. I'll trade you my lion skin for the skull if you want," Denny said.

Huff started to answer, then stopped. This was something he obviously wanted to think carefully about. As he thought, he unconsciously pulled the lion skin around his shoulders. He liked the feel of it and the secure knowledge that he could have it in his room. On the other hand, you did not get a chance to own a murdered rustler's skull but once in your whole life. Still, if you could not keep the skull, what was the use of it?

"Okay," Huff sighed. "It's a deal. Are you sure you mean it?"

"I sure do. All my brothers have got skins like this, but not a one of them's got a skull. Where is it? I want to take it home with me now."

Huff looked at Denny. "How did you just happen to have that skin here tonight?" he asked suspiciously.

"Queer things just happen," Denny answered. "Come on. Let's get the skull."

Huff followed Denny out of the door with the mountain lion skin in his arms.

"Did you put Denny up to that?" Joe asked his mother with a grin.

"Both of them are happier than they were before, aren't they?" Mrs. Cutler answered. "Besides, Mrs. Hansen told

me the other day she'd be glad if Huff had a skin like that."

Joe gave her a rough pat on the back the way he would another player on the basketball team who had just made a difficult basket. Then he sat down at the table and idly looked at one of the old papers from Swink's store.

"Are any of them interesting?" he asked.

"Sure, they all are. They remind me of the old days," Grandpa said.

Joe realized that these things must have meant a lot to his grandfather. The old man had not said a word to the boys all evening. To see what was so fascinating, he picked up a pile that Grandpa had not gone through yet. It was a small bundle tied together and marked "Goods Ordered."

One by one he unfolded notations in Swink's hand-writing, listing things he had ordered—candles, shirts, corset covers, blasting powder, slop jars, frying pans. Then suddenly Joe let out a yell.

"Wow, Grandpa, look at this!"

Joe jumped up and ran around the table, holding out a handwritten note for Grandpa to see. It read:

mumy & potts   *recd. $50 in advance*   HD

Attached to the note with a rusty pin was a crude drawing that could only have been a map.

"It must mean Bellyache Bill! Don't you see?" Joe cried.

"You young fellows are always sure what time of day it is before you look at the clock," Grandpa said. "What are you talking about?"

Joe tried to be patient. He showed Grandpa the note first. "This was in the bundle of papers labeled 'Goods Ordered.' It means that Swink had agreed to buy a mummy and some pots and had made a down payment on them. The guy whose initials were HD must have been somebody Swink knew. But Swink wanted to know where he could send someone else to pick up the mummy and pots, in case HD got bumped off or something. So he had him draw a map of the place where he'd left the mummy. Can't you see? It's as clear as daylight."

"Calm down," Grandpa said. "Let me look." After a while he added, "It's sure a bum map, if that's what it's supposed to be. It might be a map of how to get in from Vesper past this ranch to Canary City. I admit there was an old wagon trail that used to go just about that same way."

Joe walked back and forth in the sitting room. He was thinking intensely. "Where's that map?" he demanded suddenly.

"Right here, of course," Grandpa answered.

"I don't mean that one. I mean that big one of Mesa Verde that Mrs. Hansen bought for us when we were in the park."

"Joe," said Mrs. Cutler, "do you mean the one I took out of your Levis when you came back?"

"Yes, that must have been where I left it. Where is it now?"

"On the shelf in the laundry closet."

Joe was back in a flash with the map in his hands. He spread it out. It was a big topographical map, and it covered the whole table.

"Now give me that," he said, pointing at the drawing Grandpa still held. Holding the small drawing over the big map, he began to shift it around from one position to another. Grandpa and Mrs. Cutler moved over to watch. There were any number of Y shapes on the Mesa Verde map, similar to the Y in the drawing. All of them showed where canyons ran back into the mesas.

"I know it. I just know it. It's Soda Canyon right where we were," Joe said. "Look, Grandpa, on the map where it says Hemenway House. There are five ruins marked there.

And there are five marks right here on Swink's map. Then right across there's Balcony House, and Swink has got lots of marks there for a big place. That wavy line at the bottom is the Mancos River."

Grandpa looked carefully with his magnifying glass. "But I don't see another set of five buildings up farther on the Mesa Verde map," he said. "There's nothing that corresponds to the second set of five marks on Swink's map."

"But the ranger told us that there were lots of unexplored caves in the canyon. Maybe they only put the ones they think are really important on their map. The place where you used to camp isn't shown on the map either."

Grandpa was beginning to be convinced. "Maybe you have something there."

"See, Grandpa, it would be right in the little side canyon where you said you grazed your horses that time. Can't you remember seeing any houses when you were there?"

"Well, there might have been, at that. They must have been pretty small, though—the kind the Indians only used for storing their corn."

"Grandpa, we have to go back and look. Mom, couldn't I get off for another day or two?"

Grandpa turned to Mrs. Cutler and said, "You could spare us for a couple of days. Mrs. Hansen would be glad to run you into town for shopping, and we could take the pickup truck." Grandpa was getting excited, too. "Joe, I think I know what that varmint did the day he set me afoot. He rode right back up to the side canyon where we'd hobbled and pastured our horses. That was where the only good grass was. He took off the saddles and looked through the packs to see what he had. I'd have done that myself. They were big-looking packs for a couple of cow-pokes to be running around with on the range. When he found what he had, he cached it in the nearest easy place —which must have been a cliff dwelling right handy there."

"And he didn't camp there," Joe interrupted, "because he already had his camp in the cave that *we* found. All he took was the branding iron, which he needed for a cooking rod."

"Joe, you have me convinced," his mother said. "When do you want to go and look? I'll get Denny's sister to come over again, although I wish I could go with you. But that's out."

"May we go tomorrow?" Joe asked tentatively.

"I thought you were planning to buy your jalopy tomorrow," Mrs. Cutler said.

"Well, we could pick it up on the way back from Mesa Verde. Maybe the Grogans haven't gone to bed yet. I'll call up right now," Joe said.

CHAPTER 17   A Box of Insurance

Grandpa turned the pickup truck into the driveway beside the gas pumps, and before he had come to a stop, Joe was out of the cab. Denny and Huff leaped at the same moment from the rear of the truck where they had been seated on the comfortable padding of their bedrolls.

"There she is! Isn't she a beaut? Boy, what we can do with that old wreck!" Denny cried.

Joe's head was under the hood before the garageman came out. Grandpa had insisted that first of all the boys should test the car and see if it could be made to run. He went into the garage, and in a few minutes the man came out and called, "One of you kids come in here and get this battery. Do you know how to put it in?"

"Yes, sir," Joe called back. Then he added, "Denny, you go."

Before Denny got back, Joe was in the garage himself

borrowing tools. In a little while he had the battery in place and checked the spark plugs. He looked to see if it had oil and water.

As Joe worked, Denny handed him tools and kept talking the fine points of souping up an old jalopy. Joe listened and enjoyed the talk, but he knew that the things Denny dreamed of for the car were really just dreams right now. The important thing was to get her running. Then, when they could afford it, they would make some improvements.

Huff hung around, silent and ill at ease. He did not have any idea what Joe and Denny were talking about. He hated to show his ignorance, and he hated to be useless and left out of the excitement. Finally a bright idea came to him.

"I know one thing anyhow," he said a little belligerently to Joe. "You better put some air in these tires or we won't get very far."

"By gosh, you're right," Joe said. He had been so busy with the engine that he had not inspected the rest of the car. "We only have to roll her about ten feet to the air pump. Come on, you guys, get behind her and shove. I'll guide her."

While they were blowing up the tires, the garageman leaned in the doorway watching them with amusement. "Well, gentlemen, are you ready for petrol?" he asked genially.

"About sixpence worth, my good man," Huff said with a dramatic flourish.

"What goes on here?" said Joe. "Can't you guys talk English?"

"Give us some gas, please, mister," Denny said impatiently. "We want to see how she goes."

After the gas was in the tank, it took Joe about five minutes to get the engine running. Grandpa had come out in the meantime.

"Listen to her, Grandpa!" Joe whooped. "Isn't that beautiful?"

"I hear plenty," Grandpa shouted back. "Sounds like one of them stamp mills where they break up ore."

Joe and Denny ignored him. And for the next three-quarters of an hour Joe tinkered and tested as if he were buying a Rolls Royce. This was a little more than Grandpa had had in mind. He had decided they were getting their money's worth. Now he wanted to move on. But there was another half-hour's delay, while Joe bargained

with the garageman for a new secondhand battery, a distributor from another old car, a set of new points for it, and a better set of spark plugs. Finally he chose a secondhand tire and inner tube to replace the one that had a rip in the side wall.

"We'll fix this one up for a spare," he said. "Now we have enough money left to buy some paint."

"You can decide on the color while we're driving," Grandpa said. "I've signed the papers and paid the bills. Let's go."

All the way to the park entrance Denny and Huff argued about the color to be used on the jalopy. Denny favored the brightest red the paint store had. Huff knew the exact shade he wanted—electric blue, it was called. Neither one would compromise on a combination of the two. But Denny finally gave in, when Huff said, "You're going to have the car—let me have the color." Denny saw the logic of this and agreed. Besides he was already thinking about getting imitation leopard skin for the seat covers when they could afford to buy them.

At the entrance gate to the park, the ranger peered into the cab and then at the rear of the pickup. "Back again?" he said. "Where's the lady?"

Grandpa answered, "We came back to look for her. We decided we couldn't wait till fall when you add up those figures that show how many people get lost in these parts every year."

The closer they came to the campground, the more Joe's thoughts left the jalopy. With the steep climb up onto the mesa, he felt he was entering a totally different and totally fascinating world. The tremendous view that lay off to the north side of the mesa filled him with a sense that he could somehow do anything in the world if he wanted to. He was quite sure he would find Bellyache Bill, and it almost seemed as if he could bring the mummy back to life—just as he had made the old jalopy run.

When the truck pulled into the campground, he did not wait to unload it. He walked quickly to the cliff edge nearby. The bigness of the canyon and the sky above seemed to be part of him. The challenging puzzle of how people had once worked out their lives in this place was here to solve.

People could do marvelous things—like building up a civilization in this lonely spot, or like inventing automobiles. Amid the remoteness of this mesa, Joe felt a great new idea filling his whole being, an idea about all humans, an idea about himself. People could do amazing, important, difficult things. Life seemed suddenly enormously exciting to Joe.

"Hey, Joe!"

The call from Denny broke into his thoughts. In a minute he was back at the camp site with an armload of wood from the woodpile.

Huff was just about to drop Joe's bedroll out of the truck when Joe caught sight of him. "Don't drop that, Huff," he cried in alarm. "Wait a second, I'll help you with it."

"What's in there—eggs?"

Joe ignored the question and set the bedroll down without jarring it. Huff knew better than to keep on asking, but he was determined to be nearby when Joe opened up his blankets.

"Now, Joe, you get the chuck box out of the truck," Grandpa said. "I'm going to drive to headquarters and give them fair warning that you boys are loose in the park again. You better start supper while I'm gone."

Something in the old man's voice indicated that he felt he might have some trouble getting permission for their trip in search of the mummy. Joe had thought of the same thing. But if they ran into difficulties, he had worked out a plan he hoped would save the day. Still, he could not help worrying a little as he built the fire and got the beefsteak ready to fry. Huff and Denny opened canned tomatoes and canned peaches.

Grandpa was gone for some time. While they waited, they dug hip-holes in the hard-baked clay. When Joe carefully unrolled his blankets, Huff was right beside him, watching owlishly. A tin cake box was in the center of the bedroll. For a moment Joe seemed uncertain what to do with it. Huff said nothing, but caught Denny's eye and pointed.

"Cake!" Denny cried. "Let's have a piece while we're waiting."

"No. Your mother says cake spoils your appetite," Joe parried.

Just then Grandpa drove up and climbed out of the cab. Without waiting to hear his report, Joe put the cake box in the cab, ostentatiously locked the doors, and gave the keys to Grandpa.

"You said people never steal anything here," he said, "but I'm not taking any chances with these two characters. What did they say at headquarters?"

"They said if you get stuck again they'll just dam up the canyon and wait till it rains and let you float out," Grandpa replied. "I saw that Price fellow, and he seemed to be wishing he could take a nice quiet trip to Durango while you're in the park."

"Come on, Fibber, let's eat. I'm practically starved," Denny said.

Joe was relieved that Grandpa had apparently smoothed things over. Now he looked forward to the Indian dances and the talks about the cliff dwellings that were given every night in a kind of natural open-air theater near the campground. Tonight the speaker was going to tell about all the inventions the people who lived on the mesa had made. In the museum, Joe had seen a lot of the cliff dwellers' tools and he was fascinated by the idea that there had been clever inventors living in those ancient times, just as there were today.

When Denny finished off his last drop of peach juice, he said, "Now, Joe, how about giving us some of that cake?"

"Who said I had any cake?"

"I saw it."

"You saw a cake *box*," Joe answered.

"Well?"

"That box is where I keep our insurance—just in case we get into any more trouble with the rangers." More than that Joe refused to say.

CHAPTER 18 High and Dry

As Grandpa and the three boys crossed from the sunlight on the western side of Soda Canyon into the morning shadow on the eastern side, Joe asked a question that had been on his mind:

"Grandpa, did you tell the rangers exactly where we're going and what we're looking for?"

"What I told them was true," Grandpa answered. "I said I was going to show you the exact spot where my partner and I tethered our horses the night before they got stolen from us. We're just about there."

"That's all you told them?"

"Yep, except that I'd guarantee you wouldn't go off and get stuck some place late at night."

"Then when we find the mummy it will be a big surprise to them?"

"I'm not certain that anything you kids do would surprise those rangers now. But they sure will be interested," Grandpa said.

A little farther on, a side canyon turned off to the east. "This is what we're looking for, isn't it?" Joe asked.

"It looks like the exact same place to me," Grandpa answered.

"I don't see much grass here," Huff said. "I thought you told us that when you were here you put the horses here to graze."

"It's not exactly like the lawns you're used to in Denver," Grandpa replied. He pointed to tufts of scrawny grass. "Mountain ponies are used to stuff like that, and unless the spring farther along has gone dry, there'll be a little green grass, too."

"I still can't understand something," Joe said. "If the houses that our map shows are really there, why didn't you and your partner use them, Grandpa, instead of going on down the canyon?"

"We just didn't notice them, I guess. My partner and I had found the other place and set up a camp there—and that was that."

There was a clear view now of the canyon wall ahead. Joe's eyes scoured every inch of it. It was a discouraging prospect. The cliff seemed absolutely perpendicular, and there were no deep shadows that indicated the big caverns where cliff dwellings were built. A few streaks across the cliff ran parallel to the flat top of the mesa. Joe's eyes traced carefully along each of these. Finally, in one of the streaks about halfway down the cliff, he saw irregularities in the shading of the rock.

To get a better view, he ran across to the opposite side of the narrow side canyon and climbed the steep slope as high as he could. Huff and Denny followed him. Again Joe looked at the streak. There were definite dark squarish shapes that might be doors or windows carved in a masonry wall.

Joe could make out clearly first one of these holes, then another, then another. There were five altogether. "Grandpa! The houses are there all right. Five of them!" he shouted to the old man who had lain down to rest in the scant shade of a rabbit bush. "I've found the place! I've found it!"

"Where, Joe? Where?" Huff and Denny crowded up on each side of Joe and peered along his arm as he pointed in the direction of the ledge and the five stone walls.

"I don't see anything," Denny said.

But Huff followed Joe's instruction and moved his eyes slowly along the ledge. "You're right!" he finally said, his voice filled with admiration and excitement. "But it looks like it would take an eagle to get there."

"Don't be too sure," Joe answered. "Let's go and have a look. If that rustler lugged a mummy and pots up there, there must be an easy way."

Grandpa had started up the slope toward them. Now Joe said, "You don't have to climb to here. The houses are straight above that open place between two clumps of piñon trees. Exactly straight above," he repeated, as if he was memorizing a landmark.

"Now I guess you see why I didn't notice them when I was in here before," Grandpa said. "But I can't figure out how anybody could ever cache anything way up in there, either."

"Those houses look different from the ones at Balcony House," Denny remarked as if a sudden idea had struck him.

"A lot different," Huff added. "If you'd paid attention last night when the ranger was giving the talk, you'd know that they aren't all alike."

"Sure," Joe broke in. "Probably nobody even lived in

these. They look too small for that. The ranger said the old Indians built a lot of little tiny rooms all over the place. Probably they used some of them for corn cribs. Those houses up there would be handy for storing corn. Right here there must have been a garden," he said, sweeping his arm around to indicate the bottom of the little canyon. "Isn't that right, Grandpa?"

"I don't know. I wasn't around then. But there sure was a nice little spring they could have used for irrigation."

Joe hurried on and began to examine the cliff at close range. There was not a sign of handholds, foot-holes, a sloping edge—nothing to be seen but absolutely smooth wall.

Huff, who had listened carefully to the lecture last night, said, "Maybe the Indians got in by climbing down a rope from the top."

"That's all right for the Indians, but how did the rustler get in?" Joe answered. "There must be some awful easy way or he never would have bothered. We just have to find it."

Grandpa had stopped at the edge of the open place between the piñons. He rested there while the three boys scrambled over the broken rock at the foot of the cliff. The boys, he thought, were like nothing so much as nervous horses in a corral, trotting back and forth looking for a way out. Only this time they were all looking for a way in.

As the three of them sweated and fumed, the old man's eyes studied the little canyon. He began to wonder if his memory had been right. After all, sixty years was a long time. There was no evidence of the spring he had remembered. Of course, it was possible that it had dried up. But somehow the place seemed different, although the bottom of the canyon looked as if there was moisture there. He peered at the mound at the base of the cliff. It was curious, he thought, that there were not any trees growing there.

Except for this one spot, an unbroken row of piñons lined the cliff's base. And then he realized why. A mass of rock had obviously split away from the cliff, crushing and covering the trees at this point. Whatever path there had been for getting into the dwelling had been carried away when this mass of rock came thundering down. And the rocks had covered up the spring.

"Hev, Joe, it's no use. Come here. You can't get into

those houses and I'll show you the reason why," Grandpa called.

When Grandpa finished showing him what must have happened, Joe realized that the theory was probably right. And he was miserable.

"There's *got* to be some other way in," he said finally. "There's got to be. And I'm going to be the one that finds it."

"Well, you take a good look. We have plenty of time," Grandpa said sympathetically. "Aren't you kids starting to get hungry?"

"Aw, Joe, it's no use. We might as well go back," Denny protested.

Joe did not answer. He munched his sandwiches absentmindedly as his eyes studied every square inch of the cliff. Just above the house that was farthest to the left, he saw a kind of broad step in the cliff face, and growing on the wide ledge there was a twisted old juniper tree. From this point, down to the row of tiny houses, he guessed there was a drop of maybe fifteen feet. Would it be possible to swing down on a rope from this point? Of course it would be. But he would have to persuade the rangers to let him try to do it.

The certainty grew in Joe's mind that he would have to get special permission from the rangers, as well as some real help. He wondered whether his cake box full of insurance would do the trick.

CHAPTER 19

Denny's Half Dollar

Joe reached for his cake box, as the pickup truck pulled into the parking lot across from the headquarters building.

"It may be none of my business," Grandpa said, "but do you think it's a good idea to take cake in to a serious talk with the superintendent?"

"I'm not taking cake," Joe answered with a grin. He offered no further information. Bearing the box, he walked through the crowd of tourists in the lobby, following Grandpa who knew the route to the superintendent's office. Huff and Denny brought up the rear.

"Well, how do you do, Mr. Cutler," the superintendent said cordially. Then he looked across the room. Mr. Price was sitting there at a table. "You boys in trouble again?"

"Yes, *sir*. Bad trouble," Grandpa said a little too loudly. Mr. Price stiffened and looked up suspiciously. Then he pulled himself together and said, "Hello, boys. What's up?"

"You remember I told you about my mummy?" Grandpa said seriously to the superintendent. "You will probably find it hard to believe, but I think my grandson has traced it down. The funny thing is, we think it's right here in the park."

Then Joe and Grandpa together told the whole story of finding the clues and ending up in the canyon below the five little houses they could not reach.

"The mummy just has to be there," Joe finished. "I'd appreciate it very much if you'd let me be the one to find it. Of course, I'll have to get help. I've been thinking that Mr. Price knows so much about rope climbing and all. Maybe he and one of the other rangers would be willing to get me down into that house where the mummy is."

The superintendent looked at Mr. Price. There was dead silence. Joe waited for a moment. Then, a little nervously, he put the cake box in front of the superintendent.

"What's that, young man?"

Joe took off the lid and burrowed in a nest of absorbent cotton which seemed to fill the box. Slowly, carefully, he

lifted out the little Indian pot he had discovered in the ruins of Swink's store. As he handed it to the superintendent, Mr. Price jumped up from his table and hurried across the room. The two men in their neat green uniforms looked at the little pot from all angles and then at Joe.

"This is a beauty. Where in the world did you get it?" the superintendent asked.

Mr. Price's face was a mixture of suspicion, admiration, and caution. He said nothing.

"It really is a genuine Mesa Verde pot, isn't it?" Joe asked.

"Yes, indeed."

Grandpa saw the doubt on Mr. Price's face and said in amusement, "I know what you're thinking. No, Joe didn't swipe it from a cave around here."

Joe explained to them briefly how he had discovered the pot.

"It would be a wonderful addition to our museum," the superintendent said.

"I was thinking of that myself," Joe murmured a little self-consciously. "I thought maybe I'd give it to you, together with the mummy and the other pots that are hidden in the little house."

The superintendent laughed out loud, and even Mr. Price relaxed into a broad grin at the shrewd bargain Joe was striking.

"Well, I guess we'd better talk business about getting into the ruin," Mr. Price said. "Tomorrow is my day off, sir," he added to the superintendent. "Bim is off, too, and I think I could persuade him to go, if you will give us permission."

And so it was arranged.

Mr. Price looked at the cowboy hats Joe and Denny wore and at Huff's bare head. "Can you ride a horse?" he asked Huff.

Before Huff could answer, Joe said, "He'll make it, if the horse is gentle."

"All right," said Mr. Price. "We'll meet at the corral at seven tomorrow morning. I'll arrange for the horses and other things. You bring lunches. Will you go, too, Mr. Cutler?"

Grandpa shook his head. "This is a job for young fellows. I'll stay here and help the super run the park while you're gone."

"Horses?" Denny broke in. "What are we going to want horses for?"

"There's a good horseback trail that goes along the top of the mesa just behind those little houses," Mr. Price answered. "It's about a twelve-mile ride from here, because we have to circle way around the heads of the canyons and then come down the mesa again. It will be a lot easier all around than trying to go straight across and find a way to the top of the cliff."

"Who's arguing?" Denny said.

"Don't get fresh, Denny," said Joe. "Thanks a lot, Mr. Price. We'll be ready."

As they piled into the pickup truck outside, Huff proposed that they stop off at the Lodge on the way back to the campground. He wanted to see the Navahos there at work weaving rugs and making jewelry out of silver. On their other trip, only Mrs. Hansen had had the time to enjoy this feature of the park. The other boys were delighted with Huff's suggestion, and Grandpa readily agreed.

The Lodge was a combination of eating place and curio store. Outside it, a very tall and very dignified old Navaho had set up his silversmith shop on one side of the entrance, and on the other his wife had her loom on which she was making one of the beautiful traditional Navaho blankets.

Little bunches of tourists were gathered around both the silversmith and the weaver. Huff watched the handsome, elderly woman pass threads back and forth across the long upright strings on her loom. Joe and Denny made straight for the silversmith where the ping, ping, ping of his hammer on the anvil attracted them. The flame that leaped out of the blowtorch at his side made a rushing, windy sound. The smith, who had a band of cloth wrapped around his head, was adjusting the clasp on one of his bracelets which a tourist had just bought at the curio store inside. Joe wondered if he could ever train his fingers to do such beautiful and delicate work, and he was eager to see more of the craftsman's things.

Inside the Lodge were showcases full of belts made of conchas, bracelets, rings, brooches, and saddle decorations. Joe studied them and fingered the soft Navaho rugs on display.

Grandpa recognized a lady behind one of the counters. She was a relative of the Wetherill brothers who had discovered Mesa Verde, and he was soon in deep conversation with her.

Huff began buying postcards he wanted to mail to friends in Denver, and Denny was all eyes in front of a souvenir counter. There he saw decal stickers of Mesa Verde scenes which tourists bought and pasted in automobile windows.

Running to Joe, Denny dragged him to the counter. "Joe, we got to have some of those for our jalopy, don't you think?" he said.

Joe was bored with the idea and just shrugged. He wanted to go on looking at Indian things which interested him more.

Huff, too, turned down the proposal to buy some of the stickers. "Buy them yourself, if you want them so much," he said.

"But I haven't any money," Denny protested. "Lend me thirty cents, then."

"You still owe me a dime, and besides I need my money to buy postcards," Huff answered.

Denny felt full of frustration and rebellion. He wished that the fifty-cent piece in his pocket was not a fake. Everybody else here could buy things, and he could not. The place was full of tourists, some of them spending a great deal of money. He saw one man peel off three one-hundred dollar bills to pay for a fine Navaho rug. And Denny did not have thirty cents for stickers.

Then, if anybody had been noticing, he would have seen a new look come over Denny's face. Grandpa would have known, if he had glanced up, that mischief was brewing. As it was, he found out soon enough.

Above the murmur in the room, his ears caught the words "Confederate money." Several tourists were looking with interest toward the counter where Denny stood, somewhat embarrassed, with three stickers in his hand. The clerk was holding up a fifty-cent piece and repeating, "What do you know? Somebody in this day and age still trying to spend Confederate money! I'm afraid you'll have to give those stickers back, son. The Civil War's over."

"Well, it's a half dollar, isn't it?" Denny said, trying to carry his bluff through.

Suddenly a thin, middle-aged man among the shoppers showed an interest and moved toward the counter. "Do you mind if I look at that coin?" he said to the clerk. After glancing at it a moment he asked Denny, "Where did you get this, sonny?"

"I excavated it from some ruins," Denny answered.

There was a general chuckle from the growing audience. Joe had not noticed what was going on until now.

When he saw that Denny was at the center of a crowd, he heaved a sigh. More trouble. He met Grandpa as they both moved toward the counter.

The thin tourist pulled a folding magnifying glass from the pocket of his fancy shirt and peered through it at the coin. "I'll tell you what, sonny," he said. "I'll pay for your stickers if you'll give me this. I like to collect odd things."

Before Denny could jump at the offer, Joe broke in. "Don't you do it, Denny. Remember, we got seventy-five cents apiece for those old quarters that we dug up the other day."

The thin man looked around in surprise and annoyance. "Oh?" he said. "Well, of course, I want to do the right thing by you. Here's a five-dollar bill. Is that all right, sonny?"

Denny's round face was one big smile, and he was just about to stretch out his hand when Grandpa stepped up next to him in the growing circle of people. "If that coin's worth five dollars now, it will be worth five dollars later," he said to Denny. "Anyway, you don't deserve anything at all right now, Denny. I'm downright ashamed of you, trying to cheat the clerk and get something for nothing."

The tourist saw he had a new situation to deal with. He

turned to Grandpa and said very politely, "If you have the authority to deal with me, I'd like to talk to you. It may seem silly to anyone else, but I would like very much to have that Confederate half dollar. Perhaps we could step outside the Lodge and discuss the matter privately."

"I can listen to anything you have to say right here," Grandpa answered, bristling.

"Just to show you that I'm serious," the man said after a pause, "I'll give you this. It should certainly clear up any misunderstanding." He reached for his wallet and took out a hundred-dollar bill.

Denny was practically purple with excitement and un-self-conscious greediness.

"It sure does clear up something," Grandpa said. "It shows you're a crook, a plain, ordinary crook. You offered to buy this kid thirty cents' worth of stickers, and now you're offering him a hundred dollars. When I went to school, that made ninety-nine dollars and seventy cents you were trying to cheat the boy out of. They don't come much lower than that. Now give back the coin."

The tourist was as embarrassed as Denny had been when the salesman caught him. "There's a terrible misunderstanding," he said, looking at the ring of unfriendly faces around. "Don't you see, any money I give this boy will be just like money he has found? He's just as likely as not to lose the coin, and it's priceless."

Grandpa looked at him as steadily as if he was aiming a rifle at a coyote. "Will you give me five hundred dollars for it?" he asked.

The man's lips drew tight over his teeth, and he snapped out, "Yes."

"Well, if it's worth that after five minutes of bargaining, I know well enough it's worth more than that. You put your tail between your legs and go back wherever it is that folks have use for a man that tries to get something for nothing. It's guys like you that are spoiling kids these days."

The tourist, embarrassed though he was, did not let pride stand in his way. Obviously he would take any insult from the ferocious old man, but he was determined to have the coin. "I'll give you a check for a thousand dollars, and you may phone my bank to make sure it is good," he said.

"I can do something a lot better than that," Grandpa answered. "I can phone a man who'll know what the coin is really worth. Now, give me the half dollar and wait here if you still think you want to buy it."

The salesman who had started the whole show said importantly, "Let me take you to the phone, sir. It's in the next room."

While Grandpa was gone, Joe and Denny and Huff had to answer dozens of questions about where they had found the coin. The salesman, too, kept repeating the story to newcomers who wanted to know what the excitement was about. This was more fun than he had had in all his weeks behind the counter this summer. The coin collector, for his part, was busy trying to find friends in the crowd, which was mostly on the side of the angry old man.

At last Grandpa pushed through the door, and the crowd became silent once more as he walked toward the coin collector. The high heels of his cowboy boots as they struck the floor made the only sound in the room.

Slowly, tensely he began to recite what he had learned from the coin dealer in Durango. As he talked he studied the side of the fifty-cent piece that showed it was Confederate money. "When the rebels tried to break up the Union, they seized the United States mint in New Orleans and stole the money that was there. Then they decided that they would make some new coins for themselves. They took some regular U.S. half dollars and they shaved off one side. They left the other side as it was. On the clean-shaved side they stamped this printing of their own." He pointed to the back of the coin. "They only stamped a handful of them, and then they changed their plans. So far only four of these things have been found anywhere, and the nuts who collect them say they're worth five thousand dollars apiece."

A gasp went up throughout the room.

"I've got an offer for that much right now from a guy who isn't in the habit of beating me in a horse trade," Grandpa added. "And it's going smack in the bank to send these three numbskulls to college."

The tourist was frantic. He acted as if he were a bidder in an auction room. "I'll equal that," he almost screeched.

"You couldn't equal zero if you tried the rest of your miserable life," Grandpa said and turned toward the door. "Let's go fix our supper, boys."

When they climbed out of the pickup truck, back at the campgrounds, Denny had the same mischievous look on his face he had had when he first stood in front of the counter in the store. He pulled a small paper bag out of his pocket. Then he showed what was in it—the three Mesa Verde stickers which he had tried to buy and a lot of others besides.

"That clerk wasn't such a bad guy after all," Denny said innocently. "Look what he gave me all for nothing."

"You can't win!" Joe said.

"You mean Denny can't lose," Huff countered.

"What do you mean lose?" Denny groaned. "Now it looks like I *have* to go to college."

CHAPTER 20   Over the Top

The next morning Joe awoke just as the sun touched the tops of the juniper trees above him. The thought of what lay ahead today crowded memories of yesterday's excitement out of his mind. He was up and washed and had breakfast on the fireplace grill before any of the others were awake. But Grandpa refused to hurry. There was no sense in getting to the corral ahead of the rangers. It was just seven o'clock when he parked the pickup truck close to the place where riding horses were kept for tourists to use.

The wrangler had five horses saddled and ready. Mr. Price and his friend Bim were there, checking the cinches and tying ropes and bundles behind the cantles of their saddles.

In a few minutes they all trotted off down the road. Suddenly Joe urged his horse up beside Mr. Price. "Don't we need a pack horse or two to bring the stuff back?" he asked.

Mr. Price looked a little embarrassed. "Well," he said, "I think it'll be job enough for one day to make sure we can get down into the houses and see exactly what there is."

It seemed perfectly obvious to Joe that Mr. Price did not expect to find anything, and he felt angry and humiliated. But at least he would have a chance to prove that the mummy and pots *were* there, so he swallowed his pride and rode on in silence.

He kept out of the conversation when the two rangers wanted to know all about the Confederate half dollar. Denny and Huff were glad enough to tell what had happened at the Lodge the night before, and Joe was glad enough to let them.

His horse had an easy gait. The squeak of the saddle leather was pleasant in his ears. The mixture of warm horse smell and the cool early morning odor of the evergreen woods slowly began to fill him with a good feeling. Overhead the sky was more blue than he thought he had ever seen it. And just a few miles ahead was the great adventure he had been looking forward to. Before long Joe thought he could not remember when life had seemed so good.

Riding, just riding, was always enough to make Denny happy. Huff was thoroughly busy on his placid mount, trying to recall all the pointers Joe had given him about horsemanship To Denny and Joe, the twelve-mile ride on the level top of the mesa was no problem. But Huff could scarcely wait to get out of the saddle when Mr. Price said, "We'll turn off the path here. We must be very close to the five houses now."

In a few minutes they dismounted and tied the horses. The rim of the canyon was hidden by trees but the rangers knew that it was not far away. Huff groaned softly as he swung down from his saddle. His legs ached so that he could hardly walk at first. But soon he was with the others peering down over the edge of the precipice into the vast space below.

"It's just a little farther along here," Joe said excitedly. "See that bare spot down below, between the trees? That's directly under the five houses." Then he ran along the edge toward the place where he expected to find the way down to the ledge just above the house farthest to the right. There was a break in the straight line of the cliff edge, sure enough. Scraggly brush grew on its sloping side. Following Joe, the others scrambled down to the spot where the lone juniper tree had taken root.

"Here we are," Joe cried. "The last house is right below this tree."

Mr. Price looked warily over the edge. He could see no sign of any house below. "This place juts out farther than the cave where you say the houses are. It's going to be a job to get in. I don't know—"

"You just have to fix that fancy knot you made when you let us down out of the other cave, and I'll bet I can get in," Joe said.

Mr. Price and Bim studied the juniper tree carefully to see how much strain it could hold. At one point its roots seemed to go deep in a crevice. In spite of the thin soil, the tree was firmly anchored.

"We can take a turn around this tree with the rope," Bim said. "It looks like it's practically made to order for the job."

"I suppose so," Mr. Price replied. "I'll go down and test it out."

"Mr. Price, I'm not afraid. Let me go down, please," Joe said.

Bim broke in. "Sure, let him. After all, it's his party."

Reluctantly, Mr. Price agreed. He checked and double-checked his knot. He examined the rock under their feet to make sure it was sound and had no dangerous cracks in it. Big chunks of this rock had fallen off the cliff in the past. One newly broken boulder lay far below. Obviously a crack had opened and let it slide away. Mr. Price did not want that to happen again right now. He also looked to find a smooth, rounded place over which the rope could go. There must be no sharp edge that could cut into it. At last he said:

"Okay. Want to try it now, Joe?"

"You two kids stand way back there and don't move," Bim said to Huff and Denny. "You might scuffle something loose that would roll over the edge and give Joe a nasty bang on the head."

There was no need to warn the two younger boys. They were already frozen silent and motionless, as far back from the edge of the cliff as they could get. Not for anything in the world would they do the thing that Joe was about to do.

"Now, when you get down there, Joe, if you start yourself swinging a little bit, you should be able to get up enough momentum to carry you in onto the ledge—if there is a ledge. Whatever you do, don't grab onto a rock in the wall of one of those old houses and expect it to hold you. And don't you get out of that rope until you're on absolutely solid footing back from the edge. Better still, don't get out of it at all. But if you do get out, put a rock on your end of the rope so it doesn't swing back out where you can't reach it when you're ready to go home to Mamma."

"Okay, okay," Joe said almost irritably, "just let me get started."

"Over the top," Bim said in a calm, encouraging tone. Mr. Price and Bim paid out the rope around the juniper tree, and Joe backed to the edge. One loop of the knot was under his seat, the other across his back and under his arms. Over the rim he went, just as he had done that night in the cave. He had thought he would not be scared this time. He knew exactly what to expect. But as he slipped over the edge and the rope pressed down onto the rock, bearing his weight, he felt a flash of awful uncertainty. There was a hundred feet of brilliant sunlight between him and the sharp rocks below. As the rangers let him down, he realized that the wall in front of him was too far

away to reach. He was dangling in thin air. If the rope broke, or if it slipped out of the rangers' hands, he would be done for.

But a moment later his sense of panic disappeared. The rope was strong and the rangers knew their business. He was as safe as if he were sitting in a chair at home in the kitchen.

"Everything all right down there?" Bim called to him from above.

"Okay," Joe shouted back. Now he was down level with the stone masonry. Right in front of him was a square opening. By careful aiming, he thought he might be able to swing straight through it. But he did not dare to try. The shock of his landing might bring down the ancient masonry around and on top of him. And there was not a wide enough ledge in front of the masonry to give a sure foothold.

But just to one side of the opening in the wall Joe could see a flat triangular area of solid stone large enough to land on. In order to reach it, he would have to swing at an angle to the face of the cliff, instead of straight backward and forward as he had originally expected. But it did not matter.

"Lower me another foot," he shouted. "Okay. Now I'm going to start swinging."

"Watch it," Mr. Price called nervously. "Don't take chances."

Joe worked his weight back and forth, the way he used to do on the swing at school. Gradually he began to swing and the arc of his swing grew longer, but it was difficult to get the right angle. His body turned, and he began to spin helplessly in the air. Now he had lost all control of his movement.

"I'm swinging wrong," he called. "I have to stop and start again."

As he spun around and around he got first a glimpse of the cliff wall rising high in front of him, then the vast, sunlit emptiness of the canyon, then the wall again. His heart beat thunderously with mingled terror and fierce excitement.

After a while he came almost to a stop. Slowly, carefully, he began to pump himself again. This time he knew better how to control his swinging chair. Back and forth he went, until, as if he were going to jump from a swing, he reached out with his feet so he could land on the ledge. The tips of his toes were on the rock. They held part of his weight. He teetered there for a moment. Then suddenly he felt himself dragged back into empty space by the force of his own weight. A frightened cry swelled up out of him.

CHAPTER 21   Ordeal on the Ledge

The big loops in the knot held firm against the jerk that Joe's fall gave to the rope, and he dangled once more in space. Limp and suddenly weary, he swung for a moment, not even answering the shout from Mr. Price— "Are you all right? Are you all right?"

When he could control his voice, Joe called back as heartily as he could, "Sure, I'm okay. You just have to let the rope out about six inches more. I'll make it this time."

"I'm going to pull you up," Mr. Price called.

"No, you don't! It's simple. I have it all figured out now," Joe answered.

"Go on, give him six more inches. Give the kid a chance," Bim said calmly.

The rope went down as Joe had directed, and he began his pumping once more. This time he landed safely on the ledge and kept his balance. But where could he go from here?

The flat stones of a masonry wall rose between him and the interior of the house. The ledge in front of the building was too small for him to get around on it and climb inside. He either had to make a hole in the masonry wall or ask to be pulled back up and admit defeat. One wall more or less in the hundreds of ruins in Mesa Verde would make no great difference, he decided.

"What are you doing there? Are you okay?" Mr. Price called.

"Sure," Joe answered. "But I have some work to do before I can get clear in."

Beginning at the top of the wall, Joe pulled stone after stone out onto the ledge beside him. No clay bound the stones together here, and his task was easy. Soon he had a hole in the wall large enough for him to crawl through.

Carefully he slipped out of the loops in the rope and anchored the big knot under some of the rocks which he had lifted from the wall. Then he called up, "I'm out of the rope now. Don't pull on it. I have it anchored at this end. Now I'm going into the first house."

Through the hole he had made, Joe could see that the

first tiny, one-room house opened into the next. Perhaps all five rooms were connected. In the first room there was nothing—absolutely nothing. The second one, which was so small he had to crawl through it on his knees, was also empty. Here, back against the side of the cliff was an opening. Obviously the Indians who had built the place had not liked the idea of going from one room to another along the narrow ledge—any more than he would like it.

The bright sunlight that came through the oblong door or window in the third tiny chamber showed nothing but a few rocks that had fallen to the floor from the wall. If there had ever been anything in this place, the cowboys had certainly cleaned it out, Joe thought to himself.

"Are you sure you're all right?" Mr. Price called anxiously.

"Yes! Don't get in a rush," Joe shouted at the top of his lungs. He was not sure how well his voice would carry out of the room, up over the rock above to the group on top.

No inner opening led from the third to the fourth room. Instead of a masonry wall, there was a solid mass of rock in front of him. For a moment Joe felt trapped. How had the Indians got into this place? Then he realized that they must have come in through the small door. That meant they had used a ledge outside. But was it still there?

Joe looked through the door and saw that a ledge did run in front of the room, but it seemed terribly narrow —eighteen inches wide at the very most. That was not wide enough for comfort this high up in the air. Joe examined the room once more, hoping he would find some other passage.

With a sinking feeling, he realized what he was up against. It was plain that the first three rooms had been built in a little separate cave of their own. Room four, and possibly room five, had been built in an adjoining cave, and the solid rock between the two caves must be several feet thick at least.

There was only one thing Joe could do. He must get to the next room along the perilous little ledge. He could not help wishing there was a handrail along it. He thought of the swinging bridge back at the Rocking O Ranch. The handrail there was not really necessary. The planks underfoot were plenty wide enough to walk on without any trouble. But the rail did help. Even Mrs. Hansen was walking across the swinging bridge now, without much hesitation.

Joe slipped carefully through the door onto the ledge. He would have liked to stand up straight, with his back to the wall, and edge along sideways. But the overhanging rock came down too low for that. The easiest thing would be to go along on all fours. He did not care how he went, as long as he had a chance to look into those next two rooms. The mummy had to be in one of them.

"I'm getting closer," Joe called out, hoping the others above him would not shout suddenly and distract him as he wormed along the ledge.

"Hurry up and get that mummy," Denny yelled. "It's way past time for lunch."

The others called down words of encouragement.

Joe could see only nine or ten feet of ledge ahead of him. He could not be absolutely sure from where he was that it reached all the way to the opening into room four. Beyond that, the ledge had obviously broken away and fallen down to the rubble heap he had walked over at the foot of the cliff yesterday. If he could not get into room four, he would have to back up along the ledge. Very calmly he said to himself, "If I can crawl forward on this ledge, I can crawl backward. I'm going to try it."

Slowly, inch by inch, he worked his way forward, with

his left shoulder always rubbing on the dry masonry. It seemed to him that his right shoulder must be sticking out a foot over empty space. He had always been proud of the fact that he was not afraid to stand on a high place. But he had to admit to himself that now he was scared. Still, he did not lose his nerve. He knew that as long as he was careful he was safe.

At the end of the ledge he looked up. The doorway was right above him. If he could only stand up straight, getting through it would be easy. But the idea of having to stoop under the bulging rock above worried him. Maybe his sense of balance would not be so good that way.

"You dope!" he suddenly muttered to himself. "You're better off with that overhanging rock than without it. You've got a brace."

Gradually he rose to his knees and then, twisting sideways, he began to straighten his legs and held his hands above him. Pushing them hard against the solid rock overhead, he felt a surge of strength and confidence. This way he was solidly braced. Nothing could get him off that cliff now. He could even stand on one foot and push with one hand and still be as secure as a timber in a mine shaft. He tried it, and swung his free hand and arm into the

chamber. Next he put his free leg through the opening. Then in one blessed instant his whole weight rolled inside, through the narrow opening, and he was safe.

Joe flopped back against a side wall to rest for a moment or two.

"Joe! Joe!" came the nervous voice of Mr. Price. "You all right?"

"Yeah, yeah! Don't you blow a gasket. I'm just resting." Joe lay there a little longer and stared through the opening at the face of the cliff opposite, across the canyon. The peace and comfort after his crawl along the ledge was wonderful. He felt quiet and drowsy, and he wanted nothing so much in the world as to take a nap. For a moment he closed his eyes and imagined his head was resting on a soft pillow back at the ranch. Then he caught hold of himself. He could not go to sleep. He had to finish his search. A strange sensation, not of dreaming he was lying on a pillow, but of *being* on a pillow came over him. His head and shoulders *were* on something soft. He reached around and felt something furry.

Instantly he sprang to his knees to see what he had rolled against.

It was a big feathery bundle. It was exactly the way

Grandpa had described the wrappings around Bellyache Bill.

"He's here! He's here!" Joe shouted passionately. "I've found Bellyache Bill!"

CHAPTER 22   Something to Be Proud Of

The Huffmobile, electric blue and resplendent, pulled up with a roar in front of the headquarters building. Denny leaned out and yelled at the green-uniformed ranger standing near the entrance.

"Mr. Price! Hey, Mr. Price! Lookit—isn't she a real beaut?"

Joe climbed from the driver's seat and approached the ever-perplexed Mr. Price, who shook hands with each of the boys in turn, then hesitated for a moment. Should he order them to move the jalopy into the parking lot where it belonged, or should he usher them right in to see the superintendent who had invited them to the park as official guests? The boys made the decision for him. They charged blithely ahead toward the superintendent's office inside.

"Glad to see you," the superintendent said. "How do

you like these, Joe?" He picked up three neatly lettered pieces of cardboard from his desk and handed them to Joe. "We're going to put them in a special case in the museum."

"How do *you* like what we came here in?" Denny broke in. He led the superintendent over to the office window, pointing proudly at the brilliant jalopy. And he proceeded to tell him all about the car, while Joe read the cards.

The first one said simply: *Small Mesa Verde bowl, possibly for ceremonial use. Gift of Joseph Cutler, Vesper, Colorado.*

The second read: *Large jar and a plate discovered in Soda Canyon by Joseph Cutler.*

The third card read:

"BELLYACHE BILL"

This mummy of a grown man was first discovered by Lyman Cutler, cowboy and early settler, who was in the vicinity branding stray calves that belonged to the Rocking O Ranch near Vesper, Colorado. Immediately after the find, an unknown horse thief stole Mr. Cutler's horses on which he had packed the mummy and the beautiful specimens of pottery also displayed in this case. Through the persistence and ingenuity of Mr. Cutler's grandson, Joseph Cutler, aged 15, the material in this case was traced to the spot where the horse thief had hidden it in another dwelling that was later rendered almost inaccessible. With remarkable courage, Joseph Cutler himself descended by rope into the dwelling and helped in the delicate task of recovering the find.

"Are they all right, Joe?" the superintendent asked, turning back from the window. "We tried to get in the whole story, except for the fancy details about hoisting you and Bellyache Bill out of the cave."

"Gee, I didn't expect this," Joe murmured, and for a minute he was too filled with emotion to say anything else.

Huff took the cards and read them. "You've got one thing wrong here," he remarked. "Joe's sixteen now. That's how come he has a license to drive our jalopy around."

"There's something else, too," Joe said. "You ought to mention Huff and Denny on the cards. They were in on the whole thing."

"You're right," the superintendent said. "We can fix that up very easily. And we want to. You boys have done a job here that you can be proud of all the rest of your lives."